A FATHER FOR
HER TRIPLETS

A FATHER FOR HER TRIPLETS

BY

SUSAN MEIER

First published in Great Britain 2013
by Mills & Boon, an imprint of Harlequin (UK) Limited.
Large Print edition 2013
Harlequin (UK) Limited, Eton House,
18-24 Paradise Road, Richmond, Surrey TW9 1SR

© Linda Susan Meier 2013

ISBN: 978 0 263 23684 2

Printed and bound in Great Britain
by CPI Antony Rowe, Chippenham, Wiltshire

For the real Owen, Helaina and Claire…
Thanks for being so adorable
I had to write about you.

CHAPTER ONE

THE BEST PART OF BEING rich was, of course, the toys. There wasn't anything Wyatt McKenzie wanted that he didn't have.

Gliding along the winding road that led to Newland, Maryland, on a warm April morning, he revved the engine of his big black motorcycle and grinned. He loved the toys.

The second best thing about being rich was the power. Not that he could start a war, or control the lives of the people who depended upon him for work and incomes. The power he loved was the power he had over his own schedule.

Take right now, for instance. His grandmother had died the month before, and it was time to clear out her house for sale. The family could have hired someone, but Grandma McKenzie had a habit of squirreling away cash and hiding jewelry. When none of her family heirloom jewelry was found in her Florida town house, Wyatt's mother believed it was still in her house in Maryland. And Wyatt had volunteered to make the thousand-mile trip back "home" to search her house.

His mother could have come. She'd actually know more about what she was looking for. But his divorce had become final the week before. After four years fighting over money, his now ex-wife had agreed to settle for thirty percent interest in his company.

His company. She'd cheated on him. Lied to him. Tried to undermine his authority. And she got thirty percent of everything *he'd* worked for? It wasn't right.

But it also hurt. They'd been married for four years before the trouble started. He'd thought she was happy.

He needed some time to get over his anger with her and the hurt, so he could get on with the rest of his life. Looking for jewelry a thousand miles away was as good an excuse as any to take a break, relax and forget about the past.

So he'd given himself an entire month vacation simply by telling his assistant he was leaving and wouldn't be back for four weeks. He didn't have to remind Arnie that his gram had died. He didn't have to say his divorce was final. He didn't have to make any excuse or give any reason at all. He just said, "I'm going. See you next month."

He revved the engine again as he swung the bike off the highway and onto the exit ramp for Newland, the town he'd grown up in. After buying the company that published his graphic novels, he'd moved his whole family to Florida to enjoy life in the sun. His parents had made trips home. Gram had spent entire summers here. But Wyatt hadn't even been home for a visit in fifteen long years. Now, he was back. A changed man. A *rich* man. Not the geeky kid everybody "liked" but sort of made fun of. Not the skinny nerd who never got picked for the team in gym class. But a six-foot-one, two-hundred-pound guy who not only worked out, he'd also turned his geekiness into a fortune.

He laughed. He could only imagine the reception he was about to get.

Two sweeping turns took him to Main Street, then one final turn took him to his grandmother's street. He saw the aging Cape Cod immediately. Gables and blue shutters accented the white siding. A row of overgrown hedges bordered the driveway, giving a measure of privacy from the almost identical Cape Cod next door. The setup was cute. Simple. But that was the way everybody in Newland lived. Simply. They had nice, quiet lives. Not like the hustle and bustle of work and entertainment—cocktail parties and picnics, Jet Skis and fund-raisers— he and his family lived with on the Gulf Coast.

He roared into the driveway and cut the engine. After tucking his helmet under his arm, he rummaged in his shirt pocket for his sunglasses. He slid them on, walked to the old-fashioned wooden garage door and yanked it open with a grunt. No lock or automatic garage door for his grandmother. Newland was safe as well as quiet. Another thing very different from where he currently lived. The safety of a small town. Knowing your neighbors. Liking your neighbors.

He missed that.

The stale scent of a closed-up garage wafted out to him, and he waved it away as he strode back to his bike.

"Hey, Mithter."

He stopped, glanced around. Not seeing any-body, he headed to his bike again.

"Hey, Mithter."

This time the voice was louder. When he stopped, he followed the sound of the little-boy lisp and found himself looking into the big brown eyes of a kid who couldn't have been more than four years old. Standing in a small gap in the hedges, he grinned up at Wyatt.

"Hi."

"Hey, kid."

"Is that your bike?"

"Yeah." Wyatt took the two steps over to the little boy and pulled back the hedge so he could see him. His light brown hair was cut short and spiked out in a few directions. Smudges of dirt stained his T-shirt. His pants hung on skinny hips.

He craned his head back and blinked up at Wyatt. "Can I have a wide?"

"A wide?"

He pointed at the bike. "A wide."

"Oh, you mean *ride*." He looked at his motor-cycle. "Um." He'd never taken a kid on his bike. Hell, he was barely ever around kids—except the children of his staff when they had company outings.

"O-wen…"

The lyrical voice floated over to Wyatt and his breath stalled.

Missy. Missy Johnson. Prettiest girl in his high school. Granddaughter of his gram's next-door neighbor. The girl he'd coached through remedial algebra just for the chance to sit close to her.

"Owen! Honey? Where are you?"

Soft and melodious, her sweet voice went through Wyatt like the first breeze of spring.

He glanced down at the kid. "I take it you're Owen."

The little boy grinned up at him.

The hedge shuffled a bit and suddenly there she stood, her long yellow hair caught in a pony-tail.

In the past fifteen years, he'd changed every-thing about himself, while she looked to have been frozen in time. Her blue-gray eyes sparkled beneath thick black lashes. Her full lips bowed upward as naturally as breathing. Her peaches and cream complexion glowed like a teenager's even though she was thirty-three. A blue T-shirt and jeans shorts accented her small waist and round hips. The legs below her shorts were as perfect as they'd been when she was cheering for the Newland High football team.

Memories made his blood rush hot through his veins. They'd gotten to know each other because their grandmothers were next-door neighbors. And though she was prom queen, homecoming queen, snowball queen and head cheerleader and he was the king of the geeks, he'd wanted to kiss her from the time he was twelve.

Man, he'd had a crush on her.

She gave him a dubious look. "Can I help you?"

She didn't know who he was?

He grinned. That was priceless. Perfect.

"You don't remember me?"

"Should I?"

"Well, I was the reason you passed remedial algebra."

Her eyes narrowed. She pondered for a second. Then she gasped. "Wyatt?"

He rocked back on his heels with a chuckle. "In the flesh."

Her gaze fell to his black leather jacket and

jeans, as well as the black helmet he held under his arm.

She frowned, as if unable to reconcile the sexy rebel he now dressed like with the geek she knew in high school. "Wyatt?"

Taking off his sunglasses so she could get a better look at his face, he laughed. "I've sort of changed."

She gave him another quick once-over and everything inside of Wyatt responded. As if he were still the teenager with the monster crush on her, his gut tightened. His rushing blood heated to boiling. His natural instinct to pounce flared.

Then he glanced down at the little boy.

And back at Missy. "Yours?"

She ruffled Owen's spiky hair. "Yep."

"Mom! Mom!" A little blond girl ran over. Tapping on Missy's knee, she whined, "Lainie hit me."

A dark-haired little girl raced up behind her. "Did not!"

Wyatt's eyebrows rose. *Three kids?*

Missy met his gaze. "These are my kids, Owen, Helaina and Claire." She tapped each child's head affectionately. "They're triplets."

Had he been chewing gum, he would have swallowed it. "Triplets?"

She ruffled Owen's hair fondly. "Yep."

Oh, man.

"You and your husband must be so…" *terrified, overworked, tired* "…proud."

Missy Johnson Brooks turned all three kids in the direction of the house. "Go inside. I'll be in in a second to make lunch." Then she faced the tall, gorgeous guy across the hedge.

Wyatt McKenzie was about the best looking man she'd ever seen in real life. With his super-short black hair cut so close it looked more like a shadow on his head than hair, plus his broad shoulders and watchful brown eyes, he literally rivaled the men in movies.

Her heart rattled in her chest as she tried to pull herself together. It wasn't just weird to see Wyatt McKenzie all grown up and sexy. He brought back some memories she would have preferred stay locked away.

Shielding her eyes from the noonday sun, she said, "My husband and I are divorced."

"Oh, I'm sorry."

She shrugged. "That's okay. How about you?"

His face twisted. "Divorced, too."

His formerly squeaky voice was low and deep, so sexy that her breathing stuttered and heat coiled through her middle.

She stifled the urge to gasp. Surely she wasn't going to let herself be attracted to him? She'd already gone that route with a man. Starry-eyed and trusting, she'd married a gorgeous guy who made her pulse race, and a few years later found herself deserted with three kids. Oh, yeah. She'd learned that lesson and didn't care to repeat it.

She cleared her throat. "I heard a rumor that you got superrich once you left here."

"I did. I write comic books."

"And you make that much money drawing?"

"Well, drawing, writing scripts..." His sexy smile grew. "And owning the company."

She gaped at him, but inside she couldn't stop a swoon. If he'd smiled at her like that in high school she probably would have fainted. Thank God she was older and wiser and knew how to resist a perfect smile. "You *own* a company?"

"And here I thought the gossip mill in Newland was incredibly efficient."

"It probably is. In the past few years I haven't had time to pay much attention."

He glanced at the kids. One by one they'd ambled back to the hedge and over to her, where they currently hung around her knees. "I can see that."

Slowly, carefully, she raised her gaze to meet his. He wasn't the only one who had changed since high school. She might not be rich but she had done some things. She wasn't just raising triplets; she also had some big-time money possibilities. "I own a company, too."

His grin returned. Her face heated. Her heart did something that felt like a somersault.

"Really?"

She looked away. She couldn't believe she was so attracted to him. Then she remembered that Wyatt was somebody special. Deep down inside he had been a nice guy, and maybe he still was underneath all that leather. But that only heightened her unease. If he wasn't, she didn't want her memories of the one honest, sweet guy in her life tainted by this sexy stranger. Worse, she didn't want him discovering too much about her past. Bragging about her company might cause him to ask questions that would bring up memories she didn't want to share.

She reined in her enthusiasm about her fledgling business. "It's a small company."

"Everybody starts small."

She nodded.

He smiled again, but looked at the triplets and motioned toward his motorcycle. "Well, I guess I better get my bike in the garage."

She took a step back, not surprised he wanted to leave. What sexy, gorgeous, bike-riding, company-owning guy wanted to be around a woman with kids? *Three* kids. Three superlovable kids who had a tendency to look needy.

Though she was grateful he was racing away, memories tripped over themselves in her brain. Him helping her with her algebra, and stumbling over asking her out. And her being unable to keep that date.

The urge to apologize for standing him up almost moved her tongue. But she couldn't say anything. Not without telling him things that would mortally embarrass her. "It was nice to see you."

He flashed that lethal grin. "It was nice to see you, too."

He let go of the hedge he'd been holding back. It sprang into place and he disappeared.

With the threat of the newcomer gone, the trips scrambled to the kitchen door and raced inside. She followed them, except she didn't stop in the kitchen. She strode through the house to the living room, where she fell to the sofa.

Realizing she was shaking, she picked up a pillow, put it on her knees and pressed her face to it. She should have known seeing someone she hadn't seen since graduation would take her back to the worst day in her life.

Her special day, graduation… Her dad had stopped at the bar on the way home from the ceremony. Drunk, he'd beaten her mom, ruined the graduation dress Missy had bought with her own money by tossing bleach on it, and slapped Althea, knocking her into a wall, breaking her arm.

Her baby sister, the little girl her mom had called a miracle baby and her dad had called a mistake, had been hit so hard that Missy had taken her to the hospital. Once they'd fixed up her arm, a social worker had peered into their emergency room cubicle.

"Where's your mom?"

"She's out for the night. I'm eighteen. I'm babysitting."

The social worker had given Missy a look of disbelief, so she'd produced her driver's license.

When the social worker was gone, Althea had glared at her. She wanted to tell the truth.

Missy had turned on her sister. "Do you want to end up in foster care? Or worse, have him beat Mom until she dies? Well, I don't."

And the secret had continued....

Her breath stuttered out. Her mom was dead now. Althea had left home. She'd enrolled in a university thousands of miles away, in California. She'd driven out of town and never looked back.

And their dad?

Well, he was "gone," too. Just not forgotten. He still ran the diner, but he spent every spare cent he had on alcohol and gambling. If he wasn't drunk, he was in Atlantic City. The only time Missy saw him was when he needed money.

A little hand fell to her shoulder. "What's wong, Mommy?"

Owen. With his little lisp and his big heart.

She pulled her face out of the pillow. "Nothing's wrong." She smiled, ruffled his short brown hair. "Mommy is fine."

She *was* fine, because after her divorce she'd figured out that she wasn't going to find a knight on a white horse who would rescue her. She had to save herself. Save her kids. Raise her kids in a home where they were never afraid or hungry.

After her ex drained their savings account and left her with three babies and no money, well, she'd learned that the men in her life didn't really care if kids were frightened and/or hungry. And the only person with the power to fix that was her.

So she had.

But she would never, ever trust a man again.

Not even sweet Wyatt.

Wyatt walked through the back door of his gram's house, totally confused.

Somehow in his memory he'd kept Missy an eighteen-year-old beauty queen. She might still look like an eighteen-year-old beauty queen, but she'd grown up. Moved on. Become a wife and mom.

He couldn't figure out why that confused him so much. He'd moved on. Gotten married. Gotten divorced. Just as she had. Why did it feel so odd that she'd done the same things he had?

His cell phone rang. He grabbed it from the pocket of his jeans. Seeing the caller ID of his assistant, he said, "Yeah, Arnie, What's up?"

"Nothing except that the Wizard Awards were announced this morning and three of your stories are in!"

"Oh." He expected a thrill to shoot through him, but didn't get one. His mind was stuck on Missy. Something about her nagged at him.

"I thought you'd be happier."

Realizing he was standing there like a goof, not even talking to the assistant who'd called him, he said, "I am happy with the nominations. They're great."

"Well, that's because your books are great."

He grinned. His work *was* great. Not that he was vain, but a person had to have some confidence—

He stopped himself. Now he knew what was bothering him about Missy. *She'd stood him up.* They'd had a date graduation night and she'd never showed. In fact, she hadn't even come to his grandmother's house that whole summer. He hadn't seen her on the street. He'd spent June, July and August wondering, then left for college never knowing why she'd agreed to meet him at a party, but never showed.

He said, "Arnie, thanks for calling," then hung up the phone.

She owed him an explanation. Fifteen years ago, even if he'd seen her that summer, he would have been too embarrassed to confront her, ask her why she'd blown him off.

At thirty-three, rich, talented and successful, he found nothing was too difficult for him to confront. He might have lost one-third of his company to his ex-wife, but in the end he'd come to realize that their divorce had been nothing but business.

This was personal.

And he wanted to know.

CHAPTER TWO

THE NEXT MORNING Wyatt woke with a hangover. After he'd hung up on Arnie, he'd gone to the 7-Eleven for milk, bread, cheese and a case of beer. Deciding he wanted something to celebrate his award nominations, he'd added a bottle of cheap champagne. Apparently cheap champagne and beer weren't a good mix because his head felt like a rock. This was what he got for breaking his own hard-and-fast rule of moderation in all things.

Shrugging into a clean T-shirt and his jeans from the day before, he made a pot of coffee, filled a cup and walked out to the back porch for some fresh air.

From his vantage point, he could see above the hedge. Missy stood in her backyard, hanging clothes on a line strung between two poles beside a swing set. The night before he'd decided he didn't need to ask her why she'd stood him up.

It was pointless. Stupid. What did he care about something that happened fifteen years ago?

Still, he remained on his porch, watching her. She didn't notice him. Busy fluffing out little T-shirts and pinning them to the line, she hadn't even heard him come outside.

In the silence of a small town at ten o'clock on a Tuesday morning in late April, when kids were in school and adults at work, he studied her pretty legs. The way her bottom rounded when she bent. The swing of her ponytail. It was hard to believe she was thirty-three, let alone the mother of triplets.

"Hey, Mithter."

His gaze tumbled down to the sidewalk at the bottom of the five porch steps. There stood Owen.

"Hey, kid."

"Wanna watch TV?"

"I don't have TV. My mom canceled the cable." He laughed and ambled down the steps. "Besides, don't you think your mom will be worried if you're gone?"

He nodded.

"So you should go home."

He shook his head.

Wyatt chuckled and finished his coffee. The kid certainly knew his mind. He glanced at the hedge, but from ground level he couldn't see Missy anymore. It seemed weird to yell for her to come get her son, but...

No buts about it. It *was* weird. And made it appear as if he was afraid to talk to her...or maybe becoming an introvert because one woman robbed him blind in a divorce settlement. He wasn't afraid of Missy. And he might not ever marry again, but he wasn't going to be an emotional cripple because of a divorce.

Reaching down, he took Owen's hand. "Come on." He walked him to the hedge, held it back so Owen could step through, then followed him into the next yard.

Little shirts and shorts billowed in the breeze, but the laundry basket and Missy were gone.

He could just leave the kid in the yard, explaining to Owen that he shouldn't come to his house anymore. But the little boy blinked up at him, with long black lashes over sad, puppy-dog eyes.

Wyatt's heart melted. "Okay. I'll take you inside."

Happy, Owen dropped his hand and raced ahead. Climbing up the stairs, he yelled, "Hey, Mom! That man is here again."

Wyatt winced. Was it just him or did that make him sound like a stalker?

Missy opened the door. Owen scooted inside. Wyatt strolled over. He stopped at the bottom of the steps.

"Sorry about this." He looked up at her. His gaze cruised from her long legs, past her jeans shorts, to her short pink T-shirt and full breasts to her smiling face. Attraction rumbled through him. Though he would have liked to take a few minutes to enjoy the pure, unadulterated swell of desire, he squelched it. Not only was she a mom, but he was still in the confusing postdivorce stage. He didn't want a relationship, he wanted sex. He wasn't someone who should be trifling with a nice woman.

"Owen just sort of appeared at the bottom of my steps so I figured I'd better bring him home."

She frowned. "That's weird. He's never been a runner before."

"A runner?"

"A kid who just trots off. Usually he clings to

my legs. But we've never had a man next door either." She smiled and nodded at his coffee cup. "Why don't you come up and I'll refill that."

The offer was sweet and polite. Plus, she wasn't looking at him as if he was intruding or crazy. Maybe it was smart to get back to having normal conversations with someone of the opposite sex. Even if it was just a friendly chat over a cup of coffee.

He walked up the steps. "Thanks. I could use a refill."

She led him into her kitchen. Her two little girls sat at the table coloring. The crowded countertop held bowls and spoons and ingredients he didn't recognize, as if Missy was cooking something. And Owen stood in the center of the kitchen, the lone male, looking totally out of place.

Missy motioned toward the table. "Have a seat."

Wyatt pulled a chair away from the table. The two little girls peeked up from their coloring books and grinned, but went back to their work without saying anything. Missy walked over with the coffeepot and filled his cup.

"So what are you cooking?"

"Gum paste."

That didn't sound very appetizing. "Gum paste?"

Taking the coffeepot back to the counter, she said, "To make flowers to decorate a cake."

"That's right. You used to bake cakes for the diner."

"That's how I could afford my clothes."

He sniffed. "Oh, come on. Your dad owns the diner. Everybody knew you guys were rolling in money."

She turned away. Her voice chilled as she said, "My dad still made me work for what I wanted." But when she faced him again, she was smiling.

Confused, but not about to get into something that might ruin their nice conversation, Wyatt motioned to the counter. "So who is this cake for?"

"It's a wedding cake. Bride's from Frederick. It's a big fancy, splashy wedding, so the cake has to be exactly what she wants. Simple. Elegant."

Suddenly the pieces fell into place. "And that's your business?"

"Brides are willing to pay a lot to get the exact

cake that suits their wedding. Which means a job a month supports us." She glanced around. "Of course, I inherited this house and our expenses are small, so selling one cake a month is enough."

"What do you do in the winter?"

"The winter?"

"When fewer people get married?"

"Oh. Well, that's why I have to do more than one cake a month in wedding season. I have a cake the last two weeks of April, every weekend in May, June and July, and two in August, so I can put some money back for the months when I don't have orders."

"Makes sense." He drank his coffee. "I guess I better get going."

She smiled slightly. "You never said what brings you home."

Not sure if she was trying to keep him here with mindless conversation or genuinely curious, he shrugged. "The family jewels."

Missy laughed.

"Apparently my grandmother had some necklaces or brooches or something that *her* grandmother brought over from Scotland."

"Oh. I'll bet they're beautiful."

"Yeah, well. I've yet to find them."

"Didn't she have a jewelry box?"

"Yes, and last night I sent my mom pictures of everything in it and none of the pieces are the Scotland things."

"So you're here until you find them?"

"I'm here till I find them. Or four weeks. I can get away when I want, but I can't stay away indefinitely."

"Maybe one of these nights I could grill chicken or something for supper and you could come over and we could catch up."

He remembered the afternoons sitting on the bench seat of her grandmother's picnic table, trying to get her to understand equations. He remembered spring breezes and autumn winds, but most of all he remembered how nice it was just to be with her. For a man working to get beyond a protracted divorce, it might not be a bad idea to spend some time with a woman who reminded him of good things. Happy times.

He smiled. "That would be nice."

He made his way back to his house and headed to his grandmother's bedroom again. Because she'd lived eight months of the year in Florida and four months in Maryland, her house was still furnished as it always had been. An outdated floral bedspread matched floral drapes. Lacy lamps sat on tables by the bed. And the whole place smelled of potpourri.

With a grimace, he walked to the mirrored dresser. He'd looked in the jewelry box the night before. He could check the drawers today, but he had a feeling these lockets and necklaces were something his grandmother had squirreled away. He toed the oval braided rug beneath her bed.

Could she have had a secret compartment under there? Floorboards that he could lift, and find a metal box?

Looking for that was better than flipping through his grandmother's underwear drawer.

He pushed the bed to the side, off the rug, then knelt and began rolling the carpet, hoping to find a sign of a loose floorboard. With the rug out of the way, he felt along the hardwood, looking for a catch or a spring or something that would indicate a secret compartment. He smoothed his hand along a scarred board, watching the movement of his fingers as he sought a catch, and suddenly his hand hit something solid and stopped.

His gaze shot over and there knelt Owen.

"Hey."

He rocked back on his heels. "Hey. Does your mom know you're here?"

The little boy shook his head.

Wyatt sighed. "Okay. Look. I like you. And from what I saw of your house this morning, I get it. You're a bored guy in a houseful of women."

Owen's big brown eyes blinked.

"But you can't come over here."

"Yes I can. I can get through the bushes."

Wyatt stifled a laugh. Leave it to a kid to be literal. "Yes, you *can* walk over here. It is possible. But it isn't right for you to leave without telling your mom."

Owen held out a cell phone. "We can call her."

Wyatt groaned. "Owen, buddy, I hate to tell you this, but if you took your mom's phone, you might be in a world of trouble."

He shoved up off the floor and held out his hand to the little boy. "Sorry, kid. But I've got to take you and the phone home."

Wyatt pulled the hedge back and walked up the steps to Missy's kitchen, holding Owen's hand. Knocking on the screen door, he called, "Missy?"

Drying her hands on a dish towel, she appeared at the door, opened it and immediately saw Owen. "Oh, no. I'm sorry! I thought he was in the playroom with the girls."

She stooped down. "O-ee, honey. You have to stay here with Mommy."

Owen slid his little arm around Wyatt's knee and hugged.

And fifty percent of Wyatt's childhood came tumbling back. He hadn't been included in the neighbor kids' games, because he was a nerd. And Owen wasn't included in his sisters' games, because he wasn't a girl. But the feeling of being excluded was the same.

Wyatt's heart squeezed. "You know what? I didn't actually bring him home to stay home." He knew a cry for help when he heard it, and he couldn't ignore it. He held out her cell phone and she gasped. "I just want you to know where he is, and I wanted to give back your phone."

She looked up at him. "Are you saying you'll keep him at your house for a while?"

"Sure. I think we could have fun."

Owen's grip on his knee loosened.

She caught her son's gaze again. "If I let you go to Mr. McKenzie's house for a few hours, will you promise to stay here this afternoon?"

Owen nodded eagerly.

Her gaze climbed up to meet Wyatt's. "What are you going to do with a kid for a couple of hours?"

"My grandmother kept everything. She should still have the video games I played as a boy. And if she doesn't, I saw a sandbox out there in your yard. Maybe we could play in that."

Owen tugged on his jeans. "I have twucks."

Missy gave Wyatt a hopeful look. "He loves to play in the sand with his trucks."

He shrugged. "So sand it is. I haven't showered yet this morning. I can crawl around in the dirt for a few hours."

Missy rose. "I really appreciate this."

"It's no problem."

Twenty minutes later, Missy stood by her huge mixer waiting for her gelatin mix to cool, watching Owen and Wyatt out her kitchen window. Her eyes filled with tears. Her little boy needed a man around, but his dad had run and wanted nothing to do with his triplets. Her dad was a drunk. Her pool of potential men for Owen's life was very small.

Owen pushed a yellow toy truck through the sand as Wyatt operated a pint-size front-end loader. He filled the back of the truck with sand and Owen "drove" it to the other side of the sandbox, where he dumped it in a growing pile.

Missy put her elbow on the windowsill and her chin on her open palm. *She* might not want to get involved with Wyatt, but it really would help Owen to have him around for the next month.

Still, he was a rich, good-looking guy, who, if he wanted to play with kids, would have had some by now. It was wrong to even consider asking him to spend time with Owen. Especially since the time he spent with Owen had to be on her schedule, not his.

She took a pitcher of tropical punch and some cookies outside. "I hate to say this," she said, handing Owen the first glass of punch, "but somebody needs a nap."

Wyatt yawned and stretched. "Hey, no need

to worry about hurting my feelings. I know I need a nap."

Owen giggled.

Wyatt rose. "Wanna play for a few hours this afternoon?"

Owen nodded.

"Great. I'll be back then." He grabbed two cookies from the plate Missy held before he walked over to the hedge, pulled it back and strode through.

Watching him go, Missy frowned thoughtfully. He really wasn't a bad guy. Actually, he behaved a lot like the Wyatt she used to know. And he genuinely seemed to like Owen. Which was exactly what she wanted. Somebody to keep her little boy company.

She glanced at the plate, the empty spot where the two cookies he'd taken had been sitting. Maybe she did know a way to keep him around. Since he was in his grandma's house alone, and there was only one place in town to get food—the diner—it might be possible to keep him around just by feeding him.

That afternoon Missy watched Wyatt emerge through the hedge a little after three. Owen was outside, so he didn't even come inside. He just grabbed a ball and started a game of catch.

Missy flipped the chicken breasts she was marinating, and went back to vacuuming the living room and cleaning bathrooms. When she was done, Owen and Wyatt were sitting at the picnic table.

Marinated chicken in one hand and small bag of charcoal briquettes in the other, she raced out to the backyard. "You wouldn't want to help me light the briquettes for the grill, would you?"

Wyatt got up from the table. "Sure." Grabbing the bag from her arm, he chuckled. "I didn't know anybody still used these things."

"It's cheaper than a gas grill."

He poured some into the belly of the grill. "I suppose." He caught her gaze. "Got a match?"

She went inside and returned with igniting fluid and the long slender lighter she used for candles.

He turned the can of lighter fluid over in his hand. "I forgot about this. We'll have a fire for you in fifteen minutes."

"If it takes you any longer, you're a girl."

He laughed. "So we're back to high school taunts."

"If the shoe fits. By the way, I've marinated enough chicken for an army and I'm making grilled veggies, if you want to join us for dinner."

"I think if I get the fire going, you owe me dinner."

She smiled. She couldn't even begin to tell him how much she owed him for his help with Owen, so she only said, "Exactly."

She returned to the kitchen and watched out the window as Wyatt talked Owen through lighting the charcoal. She noticed with approval that he kept Owen a safe distance away from the grill. But also noticed that he kept talking, pointing, as if explaining the process.

And Owen soaked it all in. The little man of the house.

Tears filled her eyes again. She hoped one month with a guy would be enough to hold Owen until…

Until what she wasn't sure, but eventually she'd have to find a neighbor or teacher or maybe somebody from church who could spend a few hours a week with her son.

Because she wasn't getting romantically involved with a man again until she had her business up and running. Until she could be financially independent. Until she could live with a man and know that even if he left her she could support her kids. And with her business just starting, that might not be for a long, long time.

While the chicken cooked, Wyatt ran over to his grandmother's house for a shower. He liked that kid. Really liked him. Owen wasn't a whiny, crying toddler. He was a cool little boy who just wanted somebody to play with.

And Wyatt had had fun. He'd even enjoyed Missy's company. Not because she was flirty or attracted to him, but because she treated him like a friend. Just as he'd thought that morning, a platonic relationship with her could go a long way to helping him get back to normal after his divorce.

He put his head under the spray. Now all he had to do was keep his attraction to her in line.

He almost laughed. In high school, he'd had four years of keeping his attraction to her under lock and key. While she'd been dating football stars, he'd been her long-suffering tutor.

This time he did laugh. He wasn't a long-suffering kind of guy anymore. He was a guy who got what he wanted. He liked her. He wanted her. And he was now free. It might be a little difficult telling his grown-up, spoiled self he couldn't have her....

But maybe he needed some practice with not getting his own way? His divorce had shown him, and several lawyers, that he wasn't fond of compromise. And he absolutely, positively didn't like not getting his own way.

He really did need a lesson in compromise. In stepping back. In being honorable.

Doing good things for Missy, and *not* acting on his attraction, might be the lesson in self-discipline and control he needed.

Especially since he had no intention of getting married again. The financial loss he'd suffered in his divorce was a setback. He would recover from that with his brains and talent. The hurt? That was a different story. The pain of losing the woman he'd believed loved him had followed him around like a lost puppy for two years. He had no intention of setting himself up for that kind of pain again. Which meant no permanent relationship. Particularly no marriage. And if he got involved with Missy, he would hurt her, because she was the kind of girl who needed to be married.

So problem solved. He would not flirt. He would not take. He would be kind to her and her kids. And expect nothing, want nothing, in return.

And hopefully, he'd get his inner nice guy back.

When he returned to Missy's backyard in a clean T-shirt, shorts and flip-flops, she had the veggies on the table and was pulling the chicken off the grill.

"Grab a paper plate and help yourself."

He glanced over. "The kids' plates aren't made yet."

"I can do it."

"I can help."

With a little instruction from her about how much food to put on each, Wyatt helped prepare three plates of food for the kids. Owen sat beside him on the bench seat and Missy sat across from them with the girls.

It honest to God felt like high school all over again. Girls on one side. Boys on the other.

Little brown-eyed, blond Claire said, "We have a boys' side and a girls' side."

Wyatt caught Missy's gaze. "Is that good or bad?"

"I don't know. We've never had another boy around."

"Really?"

She shrugged and pretended great interest in cutting Helaina's chicken.

Interesting. She hadn't had another man around in years? Maybe if Wyatt worked this right, their relationship didn't have to be platonic—

He stopped that thought. Shut it down. Getting involved with someone like Missy would be nothing but complicated. While having a platonic relationship would do them both good.

So the conversation centered around kid topics while they ate. Wyatt helped clean up. Then he announced that it was time to go back to his grandmother's house.

"To hunt for hidden treasure," he told Owen.

Owen's head almost snapped off as he faced Missy. "Can I go look for hidden tweasure, too?"

"No. It's bath time then story time then bed-time."

Owen groused. But Wyatt had an answer for this, if only because he understood negotiating. Give the opposing party something they wanted and everybody would be happy.

He caught Owen by the shoulders and stooped to his height. "You need to get some rest if we're going to build the high-rise skyscraper tomor-row."

Owen's eyes lit up as he realized Wyatt in-tended to play with him again the next day. He threw his arms around Wyatt's neck, hugged him and raced off.

An odd tingling exploded in Wyatt's chest. It was the first time in his life he'd been close enough to a child to get a hug. And the sensation was amazing. It made him feel strong, protec-tive…wanted. But in a way he'd never felt be-fore. His decision to be around this little family strengthened. He could help Owen, and being around Owen and Missy and the girls could help him remember he didn't always need to get his own way.

It was win-win.

Missy sighed with contentment. "Thanks."

"You're welcome."

With the kids so far ahead of her, she motioned to her back door. "Sorry, but I've got to get in there before they flood the bathroom."

Wyatt laughed. "Got it."

He walked to the hedge, pulled it aside and headed for his gram's house. He went into her bedroom again and started pulling shoe boxes filled with God knew what out of her overstuffed closet. But after only fifteen minutes, he glanced out the big bedroom window and saw Missy had come out to her back porch. She wearily sat on one of the two outdoor chairs.

Wyatt stopped pulling shoe boxes out of his gram's closet.

She looked exhausted. Claire had said they'd never had another man around, which probably meant Missy didn't date. But looking at her right now, he had to wonder if she ever even took a break.

He sucked in a breath. If he really wanted to

help her, he couldn't just do the things he knew would help him get back his rational, calm, pre-divorce self. He had to do the things *she* needed.

And right now it looked as if she needed a drink.

He dropped the box, pulled two bottles of beer from the refrigerator and headed for the hedge. It rustled as he pushed it aside.

She didn't notice him walking across the short expanse of yard to the back porch, so he called up the steps. "Hey, I saw you come out here. Mind if I join you?"

"No. Sure. That'd be great."

He heard the hesitation in her voice, but decided that was just her exhaustion speaking.

He held up the two bottles of beer. "I didn't come empty-handed." He climbed the steps, offered her a beer and fell to the chair beside hers. "Your son could wear out a world-class athlete."

She laughed. "He's a good kid and he likes you. I really appreciate you spending time with him." She took a swig of beer. "Wow. I haven't had a beer in ages."

Happiness rose in him. He *had* done something nice for her.

"A person has to have all her wits to care for three kids at once. One beer is fine. Two beers would probably put me to sleep."

"Okay, good to know. This way I'll limit you to one." He eased back on the chair. "So tell me more about the cake business."

She peeked at him and his heart turned over in his chest. In the dim light of her back porch, her gray-blue eyes sort of glowed. The long hair she kept in a ponytail while she worked currently fell to her back in a long, smooth wave. He didn't dare glance down at her legs, because his intention was to keep this relationship platonic, and those legs could be his undoing.

"I love my business." She said it slowly, carefully meeting his gaze. "But it's a lot of work."

He swallowed. Her eyes were just so damned pretty. "I'll bet it is."

"And what's funny is I learned how to do most of it online."

That made him laugh. "No kidding."

He turned on his chair to face her, and suddenly their legs were precariously close. Nerves tingled through him. He desperately wanted to flirt with her. To feel the rush of attraction turn to arousal. To feel the rush of heat right before a first kiss.

Their gazes met and clung. Her tongue peeked out and moistened her lips.

The tingle dancing along his skin became a slow burn. Maybe he wasn't the only one feeling this attraction?

She rose from her chair and walked to the edge of the porch, propping her butt on the railing, trying not to look as if she was running from him.

But she was.

She was attracted to him and he wasn't having any luck hiding his attraction to her. This attraction was mutual, so why run?

"There are tons and tons of online videos of people creating beautiful one-of-a-kind cakes. If you have the basic know-how about cake baking, the decorating stuff can be learned."

He rose from his seat, too. He absolutely, positively wanted to help her with Owen, but a platonic relationship wouldn't get him over his bad divorce as well as a new romance could. And from the looks of things, she could use a little romance in her life, too. Even one that ended.

Good memories could be a powerful way to get a person from one difficult day to the next.

He ambled over beside her. Edged his hip onto the railing. "So you baked a lot of trial cakes?"

She laughed nervously. "I probably should have. But I worked with a woman whose sister was getting married, and when she heard I was learning to bake wedding cakes she asked if I'd bake one for the wedding." Missy caught his gaze, her blue-gray eyes filled with heat. Her breath stuttered out.

He smiled. In high school he'd have given anything to make her breath stutter like that. And now that he had, he couldn't just ignore it. Particularly since he definitely could get back to normal a lot quicker with a new romance.

"Because it was my first cake, I did it for free." Her soft voice whispered between them. "Luckily, it came out perfectly. And I got several referrals."

He slid a little closer. "That's good."

She slid away. "That was last year. My trial and error year. This year I have enough referrals and know enough that I was comfortable quitting my job, doing this full-time."

He nodded, slid closer. He wouldn't be such an idiot that he'd seduce her tonight, but he did want a kiss.

But she scooted farther away from him. "You're not getting what I'm telling you."

He frowned. Her crisp, unyielding voice didn't match the heat bubbling in his stomach right now.

Had he fantasized his way into missing part of the conversation?

"What are you telling me?"

"I was abandoned by my husband with three kids. We've been as close to dead broke as four people can be for four long years. It was almost a happy accident that the first bride asked me to bake her cake. Over the past year I've been building to this point where I had a whole summer of cakes to bake. A real income."

She slid off the railing and walked away from him. "I like you. But I have three kids and a new business."

His chest constricted. He'd definitely fantasized his way into missing something. He hadn't heard anything even close to that in their conversation. But he heard it now. "And you don't want a man around, screwing that up?"

She winced. "No. I don't."

The happy tingle in his blood died. He wasn't mad at her. How could he be mad at her when what she said made so much sense?

But he wasn't happy, either.

He collected the empty beer bottles and left.

CHAPTER THREE

THE NEXT MORNING, Owen blew through the kitchen and out the back door like a little boy on a mission, and Missy's heart twisted. He was on his way to the sandbox, expecting to find Wyatt.

She squeezed her eyes shut in misery. The Wyatt she remembered from their high school days never would have hit on her the way he had the night before. Recalling the sweet, shy way he'd asked her to the graduation party, she shook her head. That Wyatt was gone. This Wyatt was a weird combination of the nice guy he had been, a guy who'd seen Owen's plight and rescued him, and a new guy. Somebody she didn't know at all.

Still, she knew men. She knew that when they didn't get their own way they bolted or pouted or got angry. Wyatt wasn't the kind to get angry the way her dad had gotten angry, but she'd bet her next cake referral that she'd ruined Owen's chances for a companion today. Hell, she might have wrecked his chances for a companion all month. All because she didn't want to be attracted to Wyatt McKenzie.

Well, that wasn't precisely true. Being attracted to him was like a force of nature. He was gorgeous. She was normal. Any sane woman would automatically be attracted to him. Which was why she couldn't let Wyatt kiss her. One really good kiss would have dissolved her into a puddle of need, and she didn't want that. She wanted the security of knowing she could support her kids. She wouldn't get that security if she lost focus. Or if she fell for a man before she was ready.

So she'd warned him off. And now Owen would suffer.

But when she lifted the kitchen curtain to peek outside, there in the sandbox was Wyatt McKenzie. His feet were bare. His flip-flops lay drunkenly in the grass. Worn jeans caressed his perfect butt and his T-shirt showed off wide shoulders.

She dropped the curtain with a groan. Why did he have to be so attractive?

Still, seeing him with her son revived her faith in him. Maybe he was more like the nice Wyatt she remembered?

Unfortunately, until he proved that, she believed it was better to keep her distance.

After retrieving her gum paste from the refrigerator, she broke it into manageable sections. Once she rolled each section, she put it through a pasta machine to make it even thinner. Then she placed the pieces on plastic mats and put them into the freezer for use on Friday, when she would begin making the flowers.

She peeked out the window again, and to her surprise, Owen and Wyatt were still in the sandbox.

Okay. He might not be the old shy Wyatt who'd stumbled over his words to ask her out. But he was still a good guy. She wouldn't hold it against him that he'd made a pass at her. Actually, with that pass out of the way, maybe they could go back to being friends? And maybe she should take him a glass of fruit punch and make peace?

When Missy came out to the yard with a pitcher and glasses, Wyatt wasn't sure what to do. He hadn't worked out how he felt about her rebuffing him. Except that he couldn't take it out on Owen.

She offered him a glass. "Fruit punch?"

She smiled tentatively, as if she didn't know how to behave around him, either.

He took the glass. "Sure. Thanks."

"You're welcome." She turned away just as her two little girls came running outside. "Who wants juice?"

A chorus of "I do" billowed around him. He drank his fruit punch like a man in a desert and put his glass under the pitcher again when she filled the kids' glasses.

Their gazes caught.

"Thirsty?"

"Very."

"Well, I have lots of fruit punch. Drink your fill."

But don't kiss her.

As she poured punch into his glass, he took a long breath. He was happy. He liked Owen. He even found it amusing to hear the girls chatter about their dolls when they sat under the tree and played house. And he'd spent most of his life wanting a kiss from Missy Johnson and never getting one.

So, technically, this wasn't new. This was normal.

Maybe he was just being a pain in the butt by being upset about it?

And maybe that was part of what he needed to learn before he returned home? That pushing for things he wanted sometimes made him a jerk.

Sheesh. He didn't like the sound of that. But he had to admit that up until he'd lost Betsy, he'd gotten everything he wanted. His talent got him money. His money got him the company that made him the boss. Until Betsy cheated on him, then left him, then sued him, his life had been perfect. Maybe this time with Missy was life balancing the scales as it taught him to gracefully accept failure.

He didn't stay for lunch, though she invited him to. Instead, he ate a dried-up cheese sandwich made from cheese in Gram's freezer and bread he'd gotten at the 7-Eleven the day he'd bought the beer and champagne. When he was finished, he returned to his work of taking everything out of his grandmother's closet, piling things on the bed. When that was full he shifted to stacking them on the floor beside the bed. With the closet empty, he stared at the stack in awe. How did a person get that much stuff in one closet?

One by one, he began going through the shoe boxes, which contained everything from old bath salts to old receipts. Around two o'clock, he heard the squeals of the kids' laughter and decided he'd had enough of being inside. Ten minutes later, he and Owen were a Wiffle ball team against Lainie and Claire.

Around four, Missy came outside with hot dogs to grill for supper. He started the charcoal for her, but didn't stay. If he wanted to get back his inner nice guy, to accept that she had a right to rebuff him, he would need some space to get accustomed to it.

Because that's what a reasonable guy did. He accepted his limits.

Once inside his gram's house, tired and sweaty, he headed for the bathroom to shower. Under the spray, he thought about how much fun Missy's kids were, then about how much work they were. Then he frowned, thinking about their dad.

What kind of man left a woman with three kids?

What kind of man didn't give a damn if his kids were fed?

What kind of man expected the woman he'd gotten pregnant to sacrifice everything because she had to be the sole support of his kids?

A real louse. Missy had married a real louse.

Was it any wonder she'd warned Wyatt off the night before? She had three kids. Three energetic, hungry, busy kids to raise alone because some dingbat couldn't handle having triplets.

If she was smart, she'd never again trust a man.

A funny feeling slithered through Wyatt.

They were actually very much alike. She'd never trust a man because one had left her with triplets, and he'd never trust a woman because Betsy's betrayal had hurt a lot more than he liked to admit.

Even in his own head he hadn't considered wooing Missy to marry her. He wanted a kiss. But not love. In some ways he was no better than her ex.

He needed to stay away from her, too.

He walked over to her yard the next morning and played with Owen in the sandbox. He and Missy didn't have much contact, but that was fine. Every day that he spent with her kids and saw the amount of work required to raise them alone, he got more and more angry with her ex and more and more determined to stay away from her, to let her get on with her life. She ran herself ragged working on the wedding cake every morning and housecleaning and caring for the kids in the afternoon.

So when she invited him to supper every day, he refused. Though he was sick of the canned soup he found in Gram's pantry, and dry toasted-cheese sandwiches, he didn't want to make any more work for Missy. He also respected her boundaries. He wouldn't push to get involved with her, no matter that he could see in her eyes that she was attracted to him. He would be a gentleman.

Even if it killed him.

But on Saturday afternoon, he watched her carry the tiers of a wedding cake into her rattle-trap SUV. Wearing a simple blue sleeveless dress that stopped midthigh, and high, high white sandals, with her hair curled into some sort of twist thing on the back of her head, she looked both professional and sexy.

Primal male need slid along his nerve endings and he told himself to get away from the window. But as she and the babysitter lugged the last section of the cake, the huge bottom layer, into the SUV, their conversation drifted to him through the open bedroom window.

"So what do you do once you get there?"

"Ask the caterer to lend me a waiter so I can carry all this into the reception area. Then I have to put it together and cut it and serve it."

By herself. She didn't have to say the words. They were implied. And if the caterer couldn't spare a waiter to help her carry the cake into the reception venue, she'd carry that alone, too.

Wyatt got so angry with her ex that his head nearly exploded. Though he was dressed to play with Owen, he pivoted from the window, slapped on a clean pair of jeans and a clean T-shirt and marched to her driveway.

As she opened the door to get into the driver's side of her SUV, he opened the door on the passenger's side.

"What are you doing?"

He slammed the door and reached for his seat belt. "Helping you."

She laughed lightly. "I'm fine."

"Right. You're fine. You're run ragged by three kids and a new business. Now you have to drive the cake to the wedding, set it up, and wait for the time when you can cut it and serve it." He flicked a glance at her. "All in an SUV that looks like it might not survive a trip to Frederick."

"It—"

He stopped her with a look. "I'm coming with you."

"Wyatt—"

"Start the SUV and drive, because I'm not getting out and you don't have another car to take."

Huffing out a sigh, she turned the key in the ignition. She waved out the open window. "Bye, kids! Mommy will be back soon. Be nice for Miss Nancy."

They all waved.

She backed out of the driveway and headed for the interstate.

Now that the moment of anger had passed, Wyatt shifted uncomfortably on his seat. Even though it had been for her own good, he'd been a bit high-handed. Exactly what he was trying to stop doing. "I'm not usually this bossy."

She laughed musically. "Right. You own a company. You have to be bossy."

"I suppose." Brooding, he stared out the window. She wanted nothing to do with him, and he wasn't really a good bet for getting involved with her. And they were about to spend hours together.

She probably thought he'd volunteered to help in order to have another chance to make a pass at her.

He flicked a glance at her. "I know you think I'm nuts for pushing my way into this, but I overheard what you told the babysitter. This is a lot of work."

"I knew that when I started the company. But I like it. And it's the only way I have to earn enough money to support my kids."

Which took him back to the thing that made him so mad. "Your ex should be paying child support."

Irritation caused Missy's chest to expand. She might have been able to accept his help because he was still the nice guy he used to be. But he hadn't offered because he was a nice guy. He'd offered because he felt sorry for her, and she *hated* that.

"Don't feel sorry for me!"

He snorted in disgust. "I don't feel sorry for you. I'm angry with your ex."

Was that any better? "Right."

"Look, picking a bad spouse isn't a crime. If it was, they'd toss me in jail and throw away the key."

She almost laughed. She'd forgotten he had his own tale of woe.

"I'm serious. Betsy cheated on me, lied to me, tried to set my employees against me. All while she and her lawyers were negotiating for a piece of my company in a divorce settlement. She wanted half."

Wide-eyed, Missy glanced over at him. "She cheated on you and tried to get half your company?" Jeff emptying their tiny savings account was small potatoes compared to taking half a company.

"Yes. She only ended up with a *third*." Wyatt sighed. "Feel better?"

She smiled sheepishly. "Sort of."

"So there's nobody in this car who's better than anybody else. We both picked lousy spouses."

She relaxed a little. He really didn't feel sorry for her. They were kind of kindred spirits. Being left with triplets might seem totally different than having an ex take a third of your company, but the principle was the same. Both had been dumped and robbed. For the first time in four years she was with somebody who truly "got it." He wasn't helping her because he thought she was weak. He wasn't helping her because he was still the sort of sappy kid she'd known in high school. He was helping her because he saw the injustice of her situation.

That pleased her enough that she could accept his assistance. But truth be told, she also knew she needed the help.

When they arrived at the country club, she pulled into a parking space near the service door to facilitate entry. She opened the back of her SUV and he gasped.

"Wow."

Pride shimmied through her. Though the cake was simple—white fondant with pink dots circling the top of each layer, and pink-and-lavender orchids as the cake top—it was beautiful. A work of art. Creating cakes didn't just satisfy her need for money; it gave expression to her soul.

"You like?"

"Those flowers aren't real?"

"Nope. Those are gum paste flowers."

"My God. They're so perfect. Like art."

She laughed. Hadn't she thought the same thing? "It will be melted art if we don't get it inside soon."

They took the layers into the event room and set up the cake on the table off to the right of the bride and groom's dinner seating. Around them, the caterers put white cloths on the tables. The florist brought centerpieces. The event room transformed into a glorious pink-and-lavender heaven right before their eyes.

Around four, guests began straggling in. They signed the book and found assigned seats as the bar opened.

At five-thirty the bride and groom arrived. A murmur rippled through the room. Missy sighed dreamily. This was what happened when a bride and groom were evenly matched. Happiness. All decked out in white chiffon, the beautiful bride glowed. In his black tux, the suave and sophisticated groom could have broken hearts. Wyatt looked at his watch.

"We have about two hours before we get to the cake," Missy told him.

He groaned. "Wonder what Owen's doing right now?"

"You'd rather be in the sandbox?"

"All men would rather be playing in dirt than making nice with a bunch of people wearing monkey suits."

She laughed. That was certainly not the old nerdy Wyatt she knew in high school. That kid didn't play. He read. He studied. He did not prefer dirt to anything.

She peeked over at him with her peripheral vision. She supposed having money would change anybody. But these changes were different. Not just a shift from a nerdy kid to a sexy guy. But a personality change. Before, he'd seen injustice and suffered in silence. Now he saw injustice—such as Owen being alone—and he fixed it. Even his helping her was his attempt at making up for her ex abandoning her.

Interesting.

White-coated waiters stood at the ready to serve dinner. The best man gave the longest toast in recorded history. In the background, a string quartet played a waltz.

Wyatt looked at his watch again. Silence stretched between them. Missy knew he was bored. She was bored, too. But standing around, waiting to cut the cake, was part of her job.

Suddenly he caught her hand and led her outside, but a thought stopped her short. "Is the wedding bringing up bad marriage memories?"

He laughed and spun her in a circle and into his arms. "Actually, I'm bored and I love to dance."

"To waltz?" If her voice came out a bit breathless, she totally understood why. The little spin and tug he'd used to get her into his arms for the dance had pressed her flush against him. His arm rested on her waist. Her hand sat on his strong shoulder. And for a woman who'd been so long deprived of male-female contact, it was almost too much for her nerves and hormones to handle. They jumped and popped.

She told herself to think of the old Wyatt. The nice kid. The geeky guy who'd taught her algebra. But she couldn't. This Wyatt was taller, broader, stronger.

Bolder.

He swung her around in time with the string quartet music, and sheer delight filled her. Her defenses automatically rose and the word *stop* sprang to her tongue, but she suddenly wondered why. Why stop? Her fear was of a relationship, and this was just a dance to relieve boredom. Mostly his. To keep it from becoming too intimate, too personal, she'd simply toss in a bit of conversation.

"Where'd you learn to dance like this?"

"Florida. I can dance to just about anything."

She pulled back, studied him. "Really?"

"I go to a lot of charity events. I don't want to look like a schlep."

"Oh, trust me. You're so far from a schlep it's not even funny."

He laughed. The deep, rich, sexy sound surrounded her and her heart stuttered. Now she knew how Cinderella felt dancing with the prince. Cautiously happy. No woman in her right mind really believed the prince would choose her permanently. But, oh, who could resist a five-minute dance when this sexy, bold guy was all hers?

His arms tightened around her, brought her close again, and she let herself go. She gave in to the rush of attraction. The scramble of her pulse. The heat that reminded her she was still very much a woman, not just a mom.

He whirled them around, along the stone path to a colorful garden. As they twirled, he caught her gaze and the whole world seemed to disappear. There was no one but him, with his big biceps, strong shoulders and serious brown eyes, and her with her trembling heart and melting knees. Their gazes locked and a million what-if's shivered through her.

What if he hadn't gone away after college?

What if she'd been able to keep their date?

What if she wasn't so afraid now to trust another man?

Could she fall in love with him?

The dance went on and on. They never broke eye contact. She thought of him being good first to Owen and then to all three of her kids. She thought of him angry when he'd jumped into her SUV. Righteously indignant on her behalf, since her ex was such an idiot. She thought of him wanting to kiss her the other night, and her already weak knees threatened to buckle. If it felt this good to dance with him, what would a kiss be like?

Explosive?

Passionate?

Soul searing?

"Excuse me? Are you the lady who did the cake?"

Brought back to reality, she jumped out of Wyatt's arms and faced the woman who'd interrupted them, only to find a bridesmaid.

Missy's senses instantly sharpened. "Yes. Is there something wrong? Do I need to come inside?"

"No! No! The cake is gorgeous. Perfect." The woman in the pink gown handed her a slip of paper. "That's my name and phone number. I'm getting married next year. The third week in June. I'd love for you to do my cake. Could you call me?"

Happiness raced through her. Her cheeks flushed. "I'd love to. But I have to check my book first and make sure I don't have another cake scheduled for that day."

The pretty bridesmaid said, "Well, I'm hoping you don't." Then she slipped back into the ballroom.

Slapping the little slip of paper against her hand, Missy joyfully faced Wyatt again.

He leaned against a stone retaining wall, watching her with hooded eyes.

"Look! I'm already starting to get work for next year."

He eased away from the wall. "Yeah. I see that."

She'd expected him to be happier for her. Instead he appeared annoyed. Her heart beat against her ribs. Surely he wasn't upset that they'd been interrupted?

She licked her lips and fanned the little slip of paper. "She hasn't tasted the cake yet. This might not pan out."

"Everybody who ate at the diner loved your cakes. You know they're good."

She grinned. "I do!"

"So you're a shoo-in."

"Yeah."

She took a breath. He glanced around awkwardly.

Then she remembered they'd been dancing. Her heart had been pounding. Their gazes had been locked. Something had been happening between them. But the moment had officially been broken.

And now that she was out of his arms, away from his enticing scent, away from the pull of their attraction, she was glad. Really. This wasn't a happily-ever-after kind of relationship. He'd be around only a short time, then he'd go back to Florida. And her divorce had left her unable to trust. Even if she could trust, she wouldn't get involved in something that might distract her from her wedding cake business. She'd never, ever find herself in a position of depending upon a man again.

She turned to go back into the country club ballroom. "It's about time for the bride and groom to cut the cake. Once they get pictures, our big job starts."

She didn't even look back, just expected him to follow her. Even Wyatt with his sexy brown eyes couldn't make her forget the night she'd sat staring at the babies' cribs, knowing she didn't have formula for the next day—or money to buy it.

She would build her business, then maybe work on her trust issues. But for now, the business came first.

CHAPTER FOUR

AFTER THE BRIDE AND GROOM cut the cake, Missy sliced the bottom layer, set the pieces on plates and the plates on trays. Waiters in white shirts scrambled over, grabbed the trays and served the cake.

Wyatt glanced around. "What can I do?"

"How about if I cut the cake and put it on dessert plates, and you put the plates on the trays?"

It wasn't rocket science, but it was better than standing around watching her slender fingers work the knife. Better than wrestling with the hunger gnawing at his belly. And not hunger for food. Hunger for a kiss.

A kiss she owed him. Had she not stood him up, their date would have ended in a kiss.

Hence, she owed him.

When the last of the cake was served, she packaged the top layer, the one with the intricate orchids, into a special box. They packaged the remainder of the uncut cake into another, not quite as fancy, one. The bride's mom took both boxes, complimented Missy on the cake, then strode away to secure the leftovers for the bride.

As the music and dancing went on, Missy and Wyatt gathered up her equipment and slid it into the back of her SUV.

Just as they were closing the door, a young woman in a blue dress scrambled over. "You made the cake, right?"

Missy smiled. "Yes."

"It was wonderful! Delicious and beautiful."

Her cheeks flushed again. Her eyes sparkled with happiness. "Thanks."

"I don't suppose you have a card?"

She winced. "No. Sorry. But if you write down your name and number, I can call you." She headed for the driver's side door. "I have a pen and paper."

The young woman eagerly took the pad and pen and scribbled her name and phone number.

"Don't forget to put your wedding date on there."

After another quick scribble, the bride-to-be handed the tablet to Missy, but another young woman standing beside her grabbed the pad and pen before she could take them.

"I'll give you my name and number and wedding date, too. That was the most delicious cake I've ever eaten."

"Thanks."

When the two brides-to-be were finished heaping praise on Missy, she and Wyatt climbed into the SUV and headed home.

He'd never been so proud of anyone in his life. He didn't think he'd even been this proud of himself when he'd bought the comic book company. Of course, the stakes weren't as high. As Missy had said, she had three kids to support and no job. He'd been publishing comic books for at least six years before he bought the company, and by then, given how much influence he had over what they published, it was almost a foregone conclusion that he'd someday take over.

But this—watching Missy start her company from nothing—it was energizing. Emotional.

"You need to get business cards."

She glanced over at him, her cheeks rosy, her eyes shining. "What?"

"Business cards. So that people can call you."

She laughed her musical laugh, the one that reminded him he liked her a lot more than he should.

"It's better for them to give me their numbers. This way they don't get lost, and I control the situation."

He sucked in a breath. She liked control, huh? Well, she certainly had control of him, and it confused him, didn't fit his plans. Probably didn't fit her plans. "That's good thinking."

"I'm just so excited. I'm already starting to get work for next year." She slapped the steering wheel. "This is so great!" But suddenly she deflated.

He peered over. "What?"

"What if all the weddings are on the same day? I can't even do two cakes a week. Forget about three. I'd have to turn everybody down."

"Sounds to me like you're borrowing trouble."

"No. I'm thinking ahead. I might look like an uneducated bumpkin to you, but I've really thought through my business. I know what I can do and what I can't, and I'd have to turn down any cake for a wedding on the same day as another booking."

He nodded, curious about why her fear had sent a rush of male longing through him. He wanted to fix everything that was wrong in her life. The depth of what he felt for her didn't make sense. He could blame it on his teenage crush. Tell himself that he felt all this intensity because he already knew her. That his feelings had more or less picked up where they'd left off—

Except that didn't wash. They were two different people. Two new people. Fifteen years had passed. Technically, they didn't "know" each other. The woman she'd become from the girl she had been was one smart, sexy, beautiful female. And how he felt right now wasn't anything close to what he'd felt when he was eighteen, because he was older, more experienced.

So this couldn't be anything but sexual attraction.

A very tempting sexual attraction.

But only sexual attraction.

She had goals. She had kids. She'd already warned him off. And he didn't want another relationship...

Unless she'd agree to something fast and furious, something that would end when he left?

He snorted to himself. Really? He thought she'd go for an affair?

Was he an idiot?

He lectured himself the whole way home. But when they had unloaded the SUV and stood face-to-face, her in her pretty blue dress, with her hair slipping from its pins and looking sexily disheveled, his lips tingled with the need to kiss her.

She smiled. Her full mouth bowed up slowly, easily. "Thanks for your help."

"Thanks for…" He stopped. Damn. Idiot. She hadn't done anything for him. He'd done a favor for her. He sniffed a laugh to cover his nervousness. "Thanks for letting me go with you?"

She laughed, too. "Seriously. I appreciated your help."

He nodded, unable to take his eyes off her. The way she glowed set off crackling sparks of desire inside him. Even though he knew he wasn't supposed to kiss her, his head began to lower of its own volition.

Her blue-gray eyes shimmered up at him. Her lips parted as she realized what he was about to do. He could all but feel the heat from her body radiating to his—

She stepped back. Smiled weakly. "Thanks again for your help."

Then she spun away and raced into the house. He stood frozen.

It took a while before he realized he probably looked like an idiot, standing there staring at her back porch. So he walked into his grandmother's house and dropped onto the guest room bed without even showering. He was tired. Crazed. Crazy to be so attracted to someone he couldn't have, and it was driving him insane that this attraction kept getting away from him.

Two minutes before he fell asleep that night, he wondered if somehow her excitement for her business had gotten tangled up in his feelings for her and morphed into something it shouldn't be.

That would really explain things for him. Normally, when he decided someone was off-limits, he could keep her off-limits. So it had to be the excitement of the day that had destroyed his resolve. That was the only thing that made sense.

The next morning he strode over to her house. Ostensibly, he'd come to get Owen to play. In reality, he had decided to test out this attraction. If it had been seeing her excitement about her

business that had pushed it over the line the day
before, then he'd be fine this morning.

Her door was open, so he knocked on the
wood frame of the screen door. "Hey. Anybody
home?"

"Come in, Wyatt."

Her voice was soft but steady. No overwhelm-
ing attraction made her breathless. In the light
of day, they were normal. Or at least she was.

Now to test him.

He pulled open the screen door. "I came for
Owen...."

Papers of all shapes, sizes and colors littered her kitchen table. But she had a pretty,
fresh, early morning look that caused his heart
to punch against his breastbone. So much for
thinking it was her excitement about her wedding cake opportunities that had gotten to him
the day before. It was her. Whatever he felt for
her was escalating.

He carefully made his way to the table. "What's
up?"

She peeked up, her blue eyes solemn, serious.
"Doing some figuring."

He sat on the chair across from hers. "Oh?"

She rose, took a cup from her cupboard, filled it with coffee and placed it in front of him.

"What I need is an assistant."

"Do you think—" Because his voice squeaked, his cleared his throat. "Do you think your business is going to pick up that fast?"

She refilled her own coffee cup and sat again. "I plan for contingencies. I don't want to be known as the wedding cake lady who can't take your wedding."

He laughed. "There's something to be said for playing hard to get...." Maybe that's why she was suddenly so attractive to him? Didn't he always want what he couldn't have? Maybe he'd only been kidding himself into thinking he was trying to get his inner nice guy back? And her playing hard to get had just fed his inner selfish demon? "Everybody wants what they can't have. You could charge more money—"

"The more cakes I bake, the more referrals I get. I don't need to be exclusive. I want to start a business, a real business. Someday have a building with a big baking area and an office."

Their knees bumped when she shifted, and her gaze jumped to his as she jerked back. Her voice was shaky when she said, "I've been going over my figures, and if I didn't save money for the winter I could hire someone."

He tried to answer, but no words formed. Mesmerized by the gaze of those soft blue eyes, everything male in him just wanted to hold her.

He frowned. *Hold her. Protect her. Save her.*

Was he falling into the same pattern he'd formed with Betsy? Once they'd started dating, he got her a great apartment, a new car. All because he didn't want to see her do without.

And he knew how that had ended.

Owen came running into the room. "I made my bed!" He jumped from one foot to the other, so eager to play that energy poured from him.

Wyatt scraped his chair away from the table. "Then let's go."

Missy swallowed and she rose, too. "Yeah. You guys go on outside. Mommy has some things to think about."

Wyatt's gut jumped again. He could solve all her problems with one call to his bank. He glanced at the papers on the table. Was it really an accident that she'd picked today, this morning, after he'd nearly kissed her the night before, to run some numbers?

He sucked in a breath. He had become a suspicious, suspicious man.

But after Betsy, was that so bad? Especially if it caused him to slow down and analyze things, so neither he nor Missy got hurt?

"Come on, O. Let's go haul some dirt."

He and Owen left the kitchen and Missy squeezed her eyes shut. Since that dance, she'd had trouble getting and keeping her breath when he was around. And she knew why. He was good-looking, but she was needy. Four years with no romance in her life, four years of not feeling like a woman, melted away when he looked at her. His dark, dark eyes seemed to see right through her, to her soul. And since that dance, every time he looked at her she knew he was as attracted to her as she was to him.

They could be talking about the price of potato chips and she would know he was thinking about their attraction.

And everything inside her would swing in that direction, too.

Luckily, she had a brain that wouldn't let her do anything stupid.

They hardly knew each other. What they felt had to be purely sexual. She had kids who needed protecting. And the only way she could truly protect her kids was to make her business so successful she'd never have to depend on a man. Keeping her eye on the ball, creating the best wedding cake company in Maryland, that's what would keep her safe, independent. Eventually, she might want a relationship. She might even marry again, if she didn't have to be dependent on a man. But it would be pretty damned hard not to become dependent on Wyatt when she was broke and he had millions.

He had to be off-limits.

No matter how good-looking he was. And no matter how much she kept noticing.

Playing with Owen cleared Wyatt's mind enough that he made a startling realization as he was eating another dry sandwich for lunch, this one peanut butter from a jar he'd found in a cabinet.

His relationship with Betsy ultimately had become all about money. But so did a lot of his relationships. He hired friends who became employees, and the friendships became working relationships. He invested in the companies of friends and those friendships became business relationships.

Because money changed things. If he really wanted his feelings for Missy to cool, all he had to do was give her money for her business. Then his internal businessman would recategorize her.

Sadness washed through him. He didn't want to recategorize her. He wanted to like her. But he ignored those thoughts. He was recently divorced. With his limited time, all he and Missy would have would be a fling. She deserved better.

Walking to the back door of his grandmother's house, he sniffed a laugh. It looked as if he'd gotten what he wanted. His inner nice guy was back. He was putting Missy's needs ahead of his.

He strode through her empty backyard, knowing the kids were probably napping. He and Missy wouldn't just have time to talk privately; they could go over real numbers to determine exactly how much money she'd need.

His heart pinched again. He kept walking. This was the right thing to do.

On her porch, he knocked on the wood frame of the screen door.

She turned and saw him.

Time stopped. Her eyes widened with pleasure. When he opened the door and stepped inside, he watched them warm with desire. Her gaze did a quick ripple from his face to his toes, and his gut coiled.

"Hey."

"Hey."

"I didn't expect you back until the kids woke up."

He scrubbed his hand across the back of his neck. Offering her money suddenly seemed so wrong. She was pretty and she liked him and he'd always liked her. The house was quiet. He could slide his hand under that thick ponytail, nudge her to him and kiss her senseless within seconds.

The very presumptuousness of that thought got him back on track. She'd already rebuffed him twice. She knew what she wanted and was going after it. She wouldn't sleep with him on a whim. No matter how attracted they were.

He needed to behave himself, think rationally and get them both beyond this attraction.

"I've been considering what you said this morning about hiring someone."

"Oh?"

"Yeah. Can we sit?"

"Sure."

She sat on the chair she'd been in earlier that morning. He sat across from her again.

"You need to buy a new vehicle. Maybe a van."

She laughed. "No kidding."

"So the way I figure this, you need salary for an assistant, day care for the kids in the morning and a new van."

She nodded. "Okay. I get it. You just talked me out of spending my winter money on an assistant. It won't work to hire an assistant if the SUV breaks down."

"Actually, that's why I'm here." He took one last look at her face—turned up nose, full lips, sensual blue-gray eyes. His hormones protested at the easy way he gave up on a relationship, but he trudged on. "Rather than you using your winter money, which isn't enough anyway, I'd like to give you a hundred thousand dollars."

He expected a yelp of happiness. Maybe a scream. He got a confused stare.

"You want to *give* me a hundred thousand dollars?"

"There are hidden costs in having an employee. I'm guessing a good baker doesn't come for minimum wage. Add benefits and employer taxes and you're probably close to fifty thousand. A van will run you about thirty thousand and I'm not sure about day care."

She rose. "You're kidding me."

"No. Employer taxes and benefits will about double your expense for an assistant's salary."

"I'm not talking about the taxes. I'm talking about the money." She spun away, then pivoted to face him again. "For Pete's sake! I don't want your money! I want to be independent."

"Your business can't stand on its own."

"Maybe not now, but it will."

"Not if you don't get an influx of cash."

She gasped. "I thought you had some faith in me!"

"I do!"

"You don't!" She leaned toward him and the hot liquid he saw in her eyes had nothing to do with sexual heat. She was furious with him. "If you did, you'd give me a few months to work through the bugs and get this thing going! You wouldn't offer me money."

"You're taking this all wrong. I'm trying to help you."

"So this is charity?" She looked away, then quickly looked back again. "Get out."

"No. I…" Confused, he ran his hand along the back of his neck. What had just happened?

"Get out. Now. Or I won't even send Owen out to play with you."

Wyatt headed for the door, so baffled he turned to face her, but she'd already left the room.

She sent Owen out to play after his nap, but she didn't even peek out the window. Confusion made Wyatt sigh as he trudged up the steps at suppertime. He opened another can of the soup he'd found in the pantry. Seeing the sludgelike paste, he checked the expiration date and with a groan of disgust threw it out.

What the hell was going on? Not only was he eating junk, things that had been in cupboards for God knew how long, but he was attracted to a woman who seemed equally attracted but kept rebuffing him. So he'd offered her money, to give them a logical reason to keep their relationship platonic, and instead of making her happy, he'd made her mad. *Mad.* Most people would jump for joy when they'd been offered money.

She should have jumped for joy.

Maybe what he needed was to get out of this house? He hadn't really cared to see a lot of the people from his high school days, but he was changing his mind. A conversation about anything other than Missy Johnson and her wedding cakes and her cute kids might be just what he needed to remind him he wasn't an eighteen-year-old sap anymore, pining over a pretty girl who didn't want him. When it came to women, he could have his pick. He didn't need one Missy Johnson.

He straddled his motorcycle and headed for the diner. He ambled inside and found the place almost empty. Considering that it was a sunny Sunday afternoon, Wyatt suspected everybody was outside doing something physical. A waitress in a pink uniform strolled over. He ordered a hot roast beef sandwich and mashed potatoes smothered in brown gravy. For dessert he ate pie.

After a good meal, he felt a hundred percent better. He hadn't seen anybody he recognized or who recognized him, but it didn't matter. All he'd needed to get himself back to normal was some real food.

He paid the bill, but curiosity stopped him from heading for the door. Instead, he peeked into the kitchen. "Hey, Monty. It's me. Wyatt McKenzie."

Missy's dad set his spatula on the wood-topped island in the center of the diner kitchen. "Well, I'll be damned."

Tall, balding and wearing a big apron over jeans and a white T-shirt, he walked over and slapped Wyatt on the back. "How the hell are you, kid?"

"I'm fine. Great." He looked around. "Wow. The place hasn't changed one iota in fifteen years."

"People like consistency."

"Yep." He knew that from running his own

company, but there was a difference between consistent and run-down. Still, it wasn't his place to mention that. "I'm surprised you don't have any of Missy's cakes in here."

Monty stepped back. Returning to the wood-topped island, he picked up his spatula. "Oh, she doesn't bake for me anymore."

"Too busy with her own cakes, I guess."

Monty glanced up. "Is she doing good? I mean, one businessman to another?"

Wyatt laughed. Having seen a bit of her pride that morning, he guessed she probably hadn't told her father anything about her business beyond the basics. Maybe he'd also made the mistake of offering her money?

"She's doing great. Three future brides corralled her when she tried to leave yesterday's wedding reception."

"Wow. She is doing well."

"Exceptionally well. She's a bit stubborn, though, about some things."

"Are you helping her?"

He winced. "She's not much on taking help."

Monty snorted. "Never was."

Well, okay. That pushed his mood even further up the imaginary scale. If she wouldn't take help from her dad, why should Wyatt be surprised she wouldn't take help from him?

The outing got him back to normal, but not so much that he braved going into Missy's house the next morning. He went to the sandbox and five minutes later Owen, Lainie and Claire came racing out of the house.

While playing Wiffle ball with the kids, he ascertained that their mom was working on a new cake.

"This one will be yellow," Lainie said.

Not knowing what else to do, he smiled. "Yellow. That's nice. I like yellow."

"I like yellow, too."

"Me, too."

"Me, too."

He laughed. He didn't for one minute think yellow was that important to any one of the triplets, but he did see how much they enjoyed being included, involved. His heart swelled. He liked them a lot more than he ever thought he could like kids. But it didn't matter. He and their mother might be attracted, but they didn't see eye to eye about anything. Maybe it was time to step up the jewelry search and get back to Tampa?

CHAPTER FIVE

WYATT THREW HIMSELF into the work of looking for the Scottish heirlooms in the mountain of closet boxes.

He endured the scent of sachets, billowing dust and boxes of things like panty hose—who saved old panty hose and why?—and found nothing even remotely resembling jewelry.

To break up his days, he played with Owen every morning and all three kids every afternoon, but he didn't go anywhere near Missy.

Still, on Saturday afternoon, when she came out of the house dressed in a sunny yellow dress that showed off her shoulders and accented her curves, lugging the bottom of a cake with the babysitter, he knew he couldn't let her go alone. Particularly since her SUV had already had trouble starting once that week.

While she brought the rest of the cake to her vehicle, he changed out of his dirty clothes into clean jeans and a T-shirt. Looking at himself in the mirror, he frowned. His hair was growing in and looked a little like Owen's, poking out in all directions. He also needed a shave. But if he took the time to shave, she'd be gone by the time he was done.

No shave. No comb. Since he usually didn't have hair, he didn't really own a comb. So today he'd be doing grunge.

Once again, he didn't say anything. Simply walked over to her SUV and got in on the passenger's side as she got in on the driver's side.

"Don't even bother to tell me one person can handle this big cake. I watched you and the babysitter cart it out here. I know better. If the caterer can't spare a waiter you'll be in a world of trouble."

She sighed. "You don't have to do this."

"I know."

"You haven't spoken to me since we fought on Sunday."

He made a disgusted noise. "I know that, too."

"So why are you going?"

He had no idea. Except that he didn't want to see her struggle. Remembering her fierce independent streak, he knew that reply wouldn't be greeted with a thank-you, so he said, "I like cake."

Apparently expecting to have to fend off an answer that in some way implied she needed help, she opened her mouth, but nothing came out. After a few seconds, she said, "I could make you a cake."

He peered over at her. In her sunny yellow dress, with her hair all done up, and wearing light pink lipstick, she was so cute his selfish inner demon returned. He'd forgotten how hard it was to want something he couldn't have.

"Oh, then that would be charity and we can't have that. If you can't take my money, I can't take your cake."

She sighed. "Look, I know I got a little over-the-top angry on Sunday when you offered me money. But there's a good reason I refused. I need to be independent."

"Fantastic."

She laughed. "It is fantastic. Wyatt, I need to be able to support myself and my kids. And I can. That's what makes it fantastic. *I can do this. You need to trust me.*"

"Great. Fine. I trust you."

"Good, because I feel I owe you for playing with the kids, and a cake would be a simple way for me to pay that back."

He gaped at her. "Did you hear what you just said? You want to pay me for playing."

She shoved her key into the ignition and started the SUV. "You're an idiot."

"True. But I'm an idiot who is going to get cake at this wedding."

But in the car on the way to the reception venue, he stared out the window. He couldn't remember the last time anybody had ordered him around like this. Worse, he couldn't remember a time a *woman* had ordered him around like this—and he *still* liked her.

He sighed internally. And there it was. The truth. He still liked her.

The question was what did he do about it?

Avoiding her didn't work. She wouldn't take his money so he could recategorize her. And even after not seeing her all week, the minute he was in the same car with her all his feelings came tumbling back.

He was nuts.

Wrong…

Really? Wrong? They were healthy, single, attracted people. Why was liking her wrong?

Because she didn't want to like him.

They arrived at the wedding reception more quickly than the week before because this venue was closer. As they unloaded the square layers with black lace trim, Missy gazed at each one lovingly. In high school, she'd hated having to bake fancy cakes for the diner, but now she was so glad she had. At age thirty-three she had twenty years of cake-baking experience behind her. And she was very, very good.

"The kids told me this one is yellow."

She peeked over at Wyatt, relieved he was finally talking. "It is. It's a yellow cake…with butter cream fondant and rolled fondant to make the black lace."

"How do you make lace?"

His question surprised her. Most people saw the finished product and didn't care how it got that way.

"There are patterns and forms you can buy, but I made my own."

He studied the intricate design. "That couldn't have been easy."

"I do things like this when you're playing with the kids."

He shot her a funny look and she turned away. The little spark of attraction she'd felt when she'd seen his scruffy day-old beard and butt-hugging jeans that morning flared again. With his sexy, fingers-run-through-it-in-frustration hair and his long, lean body, he was enough to drive her to distraction.

But she wouldn't be distracted.

Well, maybe a little. She was a normal woman and he was extremely sexy. Was it so wrong to be attracted? No. The trick would be not letting him see.

They arranged the black-and-white cake from the big square layer to the smallest layer, which had a top hat and sparkly wedding veil at the peak.

"Cute."

She stood back. "Different. I'll say that."

"You act as if you didn't know how it would turn out."

"I didn't. The bride is a Goth who wanted

something black with hints of Victorian. She told me what she wanted and I made it."

"Can you eat the top hat?"

"Yep. And the veil, too."

"Amazing."

Their gazes caught. The flare of attraction became a flicker of need. She tried to squelch it, but in four years she hadn't felt anything like this. Oh, who was she kidding? She'd never felt anything like this. Wyatt was bold, sexy, commanding. And he liked her. The real her. Not the pretend version most men saw when they looked at her. He'd seen her stubborn streak, and still helped her—was still attracted to her.

What if there really was something going on between them? Something real. He could walk away. Hell, after she'd yelled at him on Sunday he should have walked away. But he hadn't. Even though they'd had a fairly nasty difference of opinion—which they'd yet to get beyond—here they were. He was still attracted to her. She was still attracted to him.

The bride arrived in her black-and-white wedding gown with her tuxedo-clad groom in tow.

At least fourteen tattoos were visible above the bodice of her strapless gown.

Wyatt's eyebrows rose. "Different."

"Very her," Missy replied, standing beside him, off to the left of the cake, out of the way so they didn't detract from it.

He looked at the bride, looked at the cake. "You're really very good at this."

Missy's smile came slowly. Anybody could throw batter into a pan and get a cake. But not everybody could match baking ability with artistry. It was a gift. She never took it for granted.

"I know."

"I can see why you're so confident."

"Thanks."

"Someday you are going to be the best."

She laughed. There was an unimaginable joy in having something she was good at. But an even greater joy at having people appreciate it. "Thanks."

He growled and she frowned at him. "What?"

"I can never seem to say the right thing to you."

Music from the string quartet blended with the noise of wedding guests taking seats. The best man took the microphone, hit it to make sure it was live. The tap, tap, tap rolled into the room like thunder.

Wyatt caught Missy's hand. "Let's go outside."

Confused, she let him lead her through the French doors to a wide wooden deck, which was filled with milling wedding guests. Avoiding them, he guided her to the steps, and they clambered down until they stood in a quiet garden.

She looked around. She hadn't done a lot of exploring of the country clubs and other wedding venues where she took her cakes, but seeing how beautiful, and inspiring, this garden was, maybe she should.

"This is nice."

He sighed heavily. "Let's not change the subject until I get out what I want to say."

She peeked over at him, suddenly realizing how alone they were. All her nerve endings sprang to life. She'd never been attracted to a man like this. And he wasn't just nice, he was thoughtful. Or trying. When he made a mistake he wanted to fix it. He didn't just walk away.

Her thoughts from before popped into her brain again.

What if something really was happening between them? Something real? Something important? Something permanent?

"I understand why my offering you money doesn't fit your plan. But I still feel like we're not beyond the insult."

She pressed her lips together. She was right. He didn't walk away. He fixed what he broke. So different from her dad and her ex.

"What you said in the car today about being able to support yourself…I thought it was pride, but I finally get it. I see the bride-cake connection. You don't want money or help because you *know* this is going to work because you have that instinct. The thing that's going to push you above the rest. You are going to be one of the best in your business. You don't *need* help."

Her insides melted. She loved it when a bride gushed over a cake, or wedding guests sought her out to compliment her, but this wasn't just a compliment. This was Wyatt. A successful entrepreneur. Somebody who knew good work when he saw it. Somebody who saw that she had what it took to be successful.

Her blood warmed with pleasure that quickly

turned to yearning. He was gorgeous and attracted to her. Plus, he understood her. Would it be so wrong to start something with him?

It had been so long since she'd wanted something for herself, purely for herself, that she instinctively tried to talk herself out of it. She told herself it felt wrong, because she knew she had to be self-sufficient before she started anything serious with a man.

But this was Wyatt. This was a guy who understood. A guy who didn't run. A guy who fixed things. A guy who liked her and believed in her. The little voice in her heart told her to relax and let it happen.

She smiled sheepishly, not quite sure what a woman did nowadays to let a man know she'd changed her mind and was willing to go after what they both seemed to want. "Thanks for the compliment."

He sighed again, this time as if relieved. "You're welcome."

Silence settled over them. It should have been the nice, comfortable silence of two friends. But her stomach quivered and her nerve endings lit up, as if begging to be touched. She'd never before felt this raw, wonderful need, and she wished with all her might that he'd kiss her.

As if reading her mind, he stepped close again. He laid a hand on her cheek. "Missy."

His head began to descend.

She swallowed hard. Even as the sensations rushing through her begged to be explored, new fear leaped inside her. It had been four long years since she'd kissed someone.

Four years.

And she wasn't just considering kissing. What burned between them was so hot she knew they'd end up in bed sooner rather than later. With their faces mere inches apart, her heart hit against her ribs. Was she ready for this?

His mouth met hers and liquid heat filled her. Like lava, it erupted from her middle and poured through her veins. She put her hands on his cheeks, just wanting to touch him, but when his tongue slipped inside her mouth, she used them to bring him closer.

She'd never felt anything like this. The pleasure. The passion. The pure, unadulterated sensuality that left her breathless and achy.

His hands roamed from her shoulders to her

waist and back up again. Hers fell from his cheeks to his shoulder, down his long, lean back, and slowly—enjoying every smooth demarcation of muscle and sinew beneath his T-shirt—drifted up again. He was so strong. So solid. Everything inside her wept with yearning. For four years she'd been nothing but a mom. A busy mom. Right now she felt like a woman. Flesh and blood. Heat and need.

As his mouth continued to plunder hers, she pictured them tangled in the covers of her big four-poster bed. Desire whooshed through her. Everything was happening so fast that her head spun.

She thought she knew him…but did she?

He thought he knew her…but he didn't. Nobody did.

She stopped kissing him, squeezed her eyes shut. *That* was the real reason she shied away from men. Nobody knew her. Sure, Wyatt had seen her stubborn streak. He'd seen her with the kids, in full mom mode, but nobody knew about her dad. Nobody knew about the beatings, the alcoholism, the gambling that had colored her childhood and had formed who she was. And at this stage in her life, she wasn't sure she could tell anybody. Just as she was equally sure Wyatt, this Wyatt who fixed things, who probed into things, who wanted to make everything right, would never let her get away with the usual slick answers she gave when anyone asked her if she'd seen her dad lately.

Wyatt would realize there'd been trouble in her past and he'd demand she talk about it.

She stepped away. "I'm sorry. I can't do this."

He caught her hand and tugged her back. "Seems to me you were 'doing' it just fine."

She couldn't help it; she laughed. He was such a fun guy, but her past was just too much to handle. Even for him.

She slipped away from him. "I'm serious. I don't want a relationship—"

He caught her hand and yanked her back. "That's perfect, because I don't want a relationship, either."

That confused her so much she frowned. "You don't want a relationship?"

He chuckled. "No."

She pointed at him, then herself, then back at him. "Then what's this?"

"A fling?"

She blinked. A fling? While she was worried about telling him her deepest, darkest secret, he was thinking fling?

"Look, I've only been divorced for two weeks—"

She stepped back, her mind reeling. Before thoughts of her secret had ruined the moment, she'd felt things she'd never felt before. And he wanted a fling? "But—"

"But what? We're single, adults and attracted to each other. There's no reason we can't enjoy each other while I'm here."

She blinked again. The emotions careening through her didn't match up with the word *fling*. "Let me get this straight. You want to sleep with me, no strings attached, no thought of a relationship. No possibility of falling in love?"

His face scrunched. "You're making it sound tawdry."

She'd never once considered sex just for the sake of sex. Even though it solved the problem of telling him about her dad, her stomach took a little leap. He didn't want to love her. He wasn't even considering it.

He caught her shoulders and forced her to look at him. "You said that your ex leaving you with three kids and no money made you independent?"

She nodded.

"Well, think about this. Think about working for something from the time you're sixteen, and one mistake—picking the wrong person to trust—causes you to lose one-third of it. But it's about more than the money. My ex cheated on me. Lied to me. Tried to undermine me with people in the industry, saying that when she got half the company she could take over with a little bit of help, positioning herself to take everything I'd worked for. She didn't just want money. She wanted to boot me from my own company. She wanted to ruin me."

"Oh." Hearing the hurt in his voice, understanding rose in Missy, but it didn't salve the emptiness, the letdown she felt from realizing he didn't even want to *consider* loving her. It seemed in her life there'd been nobody who'd ever really loved her. At home, her dad wasn't ever sober enough to have a real emotion. Her mom stayed too busy keeping up appearances that if she kissed her or hugged her, Missy always knew it was for show, not for real. Her sister locked herself away. Like Wyatt, she'd studied. The first chance she'd gotten, she'd left.

In going along, living the lie, Missy had been alone.

Alone.

Confused.

Not wanted.

He sighed. "I just don't believe relationships last, and I don't want either one of us to get hurt."

"Sure." She understood. She really did. No one wanted to be taken for granted, and hurt as he'd been by his ex. It could be years before he would trust again.

Which was why she stepped back. "I get it."

He sighed with relief. "Good."

But when he reached for her, she moved farther away. Put a distance between them that was as much emotional as physical.

"I can't have a fling." At his puzzled look, she added, "The things you didn't factor into your fling are my kids."

He frowned. "Your kids?"

"I can't leave them to be with you and you can't…well, sleep over."

His frown deepened. "I can't?"

"No. They're kids. Sweet. Impressionable. I don't want to confuse them."

"So you won't have a fling because of your kids?"

"I don't want them confused." Tears welled behind her eyes and she struggled to contain them. She hadn't ever quite realized how alone she was until a real relationship, a real connection, seemed to be at her fingertips, only to disappear in a puff. "I don't want them involved. And until they're old enough, I'm…well, I'm just not going to…" She reddened to the roots of her hair. "You know."

"Sleep with anybody." He shook his head. "You're not going to sleep with anybody until your kids are teenagers."

"I hadn't really thought it through, but I guess that's what I'm saying." Determined to be mature about this, she held out her hand to shake his. "No hard feelings?"

He took it. Squeezed once. "Lots of regret, but no hard feelings."

She nodded, but when he released her hand, disappointment rattled through her.

She liked him. But he didn't want to like her.

CHAPTER SIX

SUNDAY MORNING, Wyatt wanted nothing more than to stay in bed. He looked at the clock, saw it was only seven, and pulled the covers over his head. Then a car door slammed and he realized he'd woken because he'd heard a vehicle pull into the drive. He bounced out of bed, confused about who'd be coming to his Gram's house at seven o'clock on a Sunday morning. But when he walked to the kitchen window and peered out, he realized the caller had parked in Missy's driveway.

Who would visit Missy at seven o'clock on a Sunday?

With a sigh he told himself not to care about her. Ever. For Pete's sake. She'd rebuffed him twice, and the night before out-and-out told him she didn't want anything to do with him. She even made him shake on it.

Did he have no pride?

He ambled to the counter, put on a pot of coffee and opened the back door to let the stale night air out and the cool morning air in.

Leaning against the counter, he waited for his jolt of caffeine. When the coffeemaker gurgled its final release, he poured himself a cup.

Turning to walk to the table, he almost tripped over Owen.

Still wearing his cowboy pajamas, the little boy grinned. "Hey."

"Hey." He stooped down to Owen's height. "What are you doing here?"

"There's a man talking to my mom."

Even as Owen spoke, dark-haired Lainie opened Wyatt's screen door and stepped inside. Dressed in a pink nightgown, she said, "Hi," as if it were an everyday occurrence for her to walk into his house in sleepwear.

"Hi."

Before he could say anything else, Claire walked in. Also in a pink nightgown, she smiled sheepishly.

Still crouched in front of Owen, Wyatt caught the little boy's gaze. "So your mom's talking to somebody and I'm guessing she didn't see you leave."

"She told us to go to our woom."

At Wyatt's left shoulder, Lainie caught his chin and turned him to face her. "He means room."

"Your mom sent you to your room?"

Owen nodded. "While she talks to the man."

Wyatt's blood boiled. For a woman who didn't want to get involved with him, she was engrossed enough in today's male guest that she hadn't even seen her kids leave.

Maybe he'd just take her kids back and break up her little party?

Telling himself that was childish, he nonetheless set his coffee cup on the counter and herded the three munchkins to the door. Missy would go nuts with worry if she realized they were gone. Albeit for better reasons than to catch her in the act, he had to take her kids back.

"Let's go. Your mom will be worried if she finds you gone."

Owen dug in his heels. "But she's talking to the man. She doesn't want us to sturb her."

His eyebrows rose in question and he glanced at Helaina, the interpreter.

Who looked at him as if he was crazy not to understand. "Yeah. She doesn't want us to sturb her."

"Sturb?"

"Dee-sturb." Claire piped in.

"Oh, disturb."

Lainie nodded happily.

Well. Well. Little Miss I-Don't-Want-A-Fling didn't want to be disturbed. Maybe his first guess hadn't been so far off the mark, after all? She might not want a relationship with *him,* but she was with somebody.

Wyatt corralled the kids and directed them to the porch.

When they were on the sidewalk at the bottom of the steps, Helaina caught his hand. "We stay together when we walk."

Claire shyly caught his other hand.

Warmth sputtered through him. He seriously wasn't the kind of guy to hang out with kids, but not only was he playing in dirt and organizing Wiffle ball games, now he was holding hands.

Owen proudly led the way. He skipped to the hedge and pulled it aside.

Lainie stooped and dipped through. Claire

stooped and dipped through. Owen grinned at him.

Wyatt took one look at the opening provided and knew that wasn't going to work. "You go first. I need to hold it up higher for myself."

Owen nodded and ducked down to slip through.

Wyatt pushed the hedge aside and stepped into Missy's backyard, where all three kids awaited him.

He pointed at the porch. "Let's go."

But only a few feet across the grass, Missy's angry shout came from the house, as if she was talking to someone on the enclosed front porch.

"I don't care who you are! I don't care what you think you deserve! You're not getting one dime from me!"

Wyatt's blood ran cold. That didn't sound like the words of a lover. It didn't even sound like the words of a friend.

Could the man in her house be her ex? Returning for money? From her? After draining their accounts?

His nerve endings popped with anger. He dropped Claire's and Helaina's hands. "Wait here."

But when he looked down at their little faces, he saw Claire's eyes had filled with tears. Owen's and Helaina's eyes had widened in fear. The shouting had scared them. He couldn't leave them out here alone when they were obviously frightened.

"Oh, come on, darlin'. You know I should have gotten this house when your grandmother died. I'm just askin' for what you owe me."

Wyatt's mouth fell open. That was Monty.

"I heard you've got a sweet deal going with this wedding cake thing you're doing. I just want what's coming to me."

"What should be coming to you is jail time!"

"Aren't you being a little melodramatic?"

"Melodramatic? You beat Mom to within an inch of her life so often I'm not surprised her heart gave out. And you beat me and Althea." She stopped. A short cry rang out.

Then Missy said, "You get the hell away from me! Now. Mom may not have wanted to call the police, but the next time you show up here I'll not only call the police, I'll quite happily tell every damned person in this town that you beat us. Regularly. They'll see that the happy-go-lucky diner owner everybody loves doesn't really exist."

"You'd never get anybody to believe you."

"Try me."

By now the kids had huddled around the knees of Wyatt's sweatpants. No sound came from the house, but the front door slammed shut. With his hands on the kids' shoulders, Wyatt quickly shepherded them to his side of the shrubs, where Monty couldn't see them.

As her father screeched out of the driveway, Missy came barreling out the kitchen door. Standing on the porch, she screamed, "Owen! Lainie! Claire!" as if she'd gone looking for them after Monty left, found them gone and was terrified.

Wyatt quickly stepped out from behind the thin leafy branches, three kids at his knees. "We're here. They came to get me to play in the sandbox."

She ran down the porch steps and gathered her children against her. "They haven't eaten breakfast yet."

"I didn't know that or I would have given them cereal. I have plenty." Not knowing what else to do, he babbled on. "Gram had enough for an army, and most of it still hasn't hit the expiration date."

She looked up at him. Tears poured from her blue eyes, down her cheeks and off her chin.

He stooped down beside her and the kids. "Hey." His heart thudded against his breastbone. What did a man say to a woman when he'd just heard that her dad had beaten her when she was a child?

Wyatt didn't have a clue. But he did have a sore, aching heart. She'd had a crappy husband and a rotten father. While he'd had two perfect parents, talent, brains and safety, she'd lived in fear.

The knowledge rattled through him like an unwanted noise in an old car. He couldn't deny it, but he didn't know how to fix it.

And the last thing he wanted to do was say the wrong thing.

He set his hand on her shoulder. "You go inside. Take a shower. I'll feed the kids."

"I'm fine."

"You're crying." He hated like hell stating the obvious, but sometimes there was no way around that. "Give yourself a twenty-minute break. I told you I have lots of cereal. We'll be okay for twenty minutes."

Owen broke out of her hug. "We'll be okay, Mommy."

Fresh tears erupted. She gave the kids one last hug, then rose. Her voice trembled as she said, "If you're sure."

"Hey, we'll make a game out of it."

Owen tugged on the leg of his sweatpants. "Can we wook for tweasure?"

Wyatt laughed. "Yeah. We'll wook for treasure."

She'd never abandoned her kids.

Never handed them over to another person just to give herself time to pull herself together. But she also hadn't had a visit from her dad in…oh, eight years?

And he'd decided to show up today? Knowing she had money in her checking account? Demanding that she give it to him?

How the hell did he know she had money?

She put her head under the shower spray. Now that she'd had a minute to process everything, she wasn't as upset as she was surprised. Shocked that he'd shown up at her house like that. But now that she knew she was on his radar again, she wouldn't cower as her mom had. She'd stand her ground. And she *would* call the police. If he touched her or—God forbid—her kids, he'd be in jail so fast his head would spin.

She got out of the shower and dried her hair. In ten minutes she had on clean shorts and a T-shirt. Her hair was combed. Her tears were dry.

She headed outside.

She expected to find Wyatt and the kids in the yard. Instead, they were nowhere in sight. When she knocked on his kitchen door there was no answer, so she stepped inside.

"Wyatt?"

"Back here."

She followed the sound of his voice to the large corner bedroom, the 1960s version of a master suite, just like the one in her house. Old-fashioned lamps and lacy curtains reminded her of the room she'd inherited herself.

But the bed was covered in boxes, and more boxes were piled on the floor. Taking a bite of cereal from a bowl on the bedside table, Owen saw her. He grinned. "Hi, Mommy."

Lainie popped up from behind the bed. Claire peeked around a tall stack of shoe boxes. "We're looking for treasure."

Missy walked into the room. "In the boxes?"

Owen said, "Yeah. But Lainie spilled her milk."

Wyatt came running out of the bathroom, holding a roll of toilet paper. "Okay, everybody stand back...." Then he saw Missy. "Hey."

She took the toilet paper from him and rushed to the other side of the bed, where rolling milk rapidly approached the edge of the area rug. She spun off some tissue and caught the milk just in time.

Wyatt rubbed his index finger across his nose. "Things look worse than they really are."

On her way to dump the milk-sodden tissue in the bathroom, she said, "What is all this?"

"This," Wyatt said, following her to the bathroom, "is everything I found in the closet."

"Are you kidding me? How'd your gram get all that in a closet?"

"She was quite the crafty packer."

"I suppose." Missy glanced around. "So it looks like you haven't found the jewelry from Scotland yet."

"Nope. And the kids were fine. Great, actually, until Lainie spilled her milk."

"She gets overeager."

He laughed. "She wants to do everything at once."

"I can take them home now."

"Why? We're having fun. And I'm actually getting through three boxes a minute."

"Three boxes a minute?"

"They open, dump, get bored and move on to the next one. And that leaves me to collect up everything they dumped, and get it back in the box. As I'm collecting, I'm checking for jewelry. At this rate I'll have this whole room done by noon."

She laughed.

And he sighed with relief. But the relief didn't last long. With her tears dry and her mood improved, he knew she'd never tell him about her dad. And he couldn't just say, "Hey, I saw Monty running out of your house this morning." It would be awkward for her, like dropping someone in an ice-cold swimming pool.

Still, he couldn't let this go. He'd been the one to tell Monty she was doing well. He'd thought he was doing her a favor. Turns out he had everything all wrong. And somehow he had to fix it.

"So what happened this morning?"

She strolled back into the bedroom and walked over to Helaina, who'd dumped out a box of panty hose.

"What is this?"

He grabbed the ball of panty hose and stuffed it back into the shoe box. "My grandmother never met a pair of panty hose she didn't want to save."

"My grandmother saved them, too. She used them as filler when she made stuffed animals or couch pillows."

"Thank God. I was beginning to think my grandmother was nuts." And he'd also noticed Missy had changed the subject. "So what happened this morning?"

She sucked in a breath, ruffling Lainie's dark

hair as the little girl picked up another shoe box, popped the lid and dumped the contents.

Bingo. Jewelry.

He swung around to that side of the bed. Beads and bobbles rolled across the floral comforter. "Well, what do you know?"

Missy caught his gaze. "Don't get your hopes up. Most of this looks like cheap costume jewelry."

He picked up a necklace, saw a chip in the paint on a "pearl."

"Drat."

"Finding jewelry is a good sign, though. At least you know it's here somewhere."

He dropped the string of fake pearls to the bed. "Yeah, well, she has three furnished bedrooms. I found clothes in the drawers in the dressers in each room. All the closets are full of boxes like these." He sighed. "Who wants to go play in the yard?"

Missy laughed. "Is that how you look for jewelry? In the yard?"

He faced her. "In case you haven't noticed, I'm sort of, kind of, the type of guy who doesn't do anything he doesn't want to do."

Shaking her head, she laughed again. "So how do you intend to find the jewelry?"

He shrugged. "Not sure yet. But I'm an idea guy. That's how I got rich." It was true. Even his writing was a form of coming up with ideas and analyzing them to see if they'd work. "So eventually I'll figure out a way to find the jewelry without having to look through every darned drawer and box in this house."

"Well, I'd volunteer to help you, but I have some thinking of my own to do today."

"Oh, yeah." He sat on the bed, patted the spot beside him. That was as good of an opening as any to try again to get her to talk to him. "I just told you I'm a good idea man. Maybe I could help you with that thinking."

"No. You and I have already been over this. Your idea to solve my financial problem was to give me money."

He remembered—and winced.

"So this morning I need to go over my books again, think through how I can get a van and an assistant."

"Why the sudden rush?"

She shrugged. "No reason." She clapped her hands. "Come on, kids. Let's go."

A chorus of "Ah, Mom," echoed around him.

He rose from the bed, suddenly understanding that maybe she didn't want to talk about her dad because the kids were around. Which meant they wouldn't talk until the triplets took their naps. "I promised them time in the sandbox."

She sighed. "They're not even out of their pajamas yet."

"How about if you go get them dressed while I clean up some of this mess? Then I'll take them when you're done."

"I do want that thinking time this morning." She blew her breath out in another sigh. "I don't know how to pay you back for being so good to them."

"I already told you it makes me feel weird to hear you say you want to pay me for playing. So don't say it again."

She laughed. Then she faced the kids. "All right. Let's go. We'll get everybody into clean shorts, then you can go out to the sandbox with Wyatt."

Owen jumped. "Yay!"

Lainie raced to the door.

Claire took her mom's hand.

Wyatt watched them go, then fell to the bed again. She'd been beaten by her dad, left by her husband with three babies, and now struggled with growing a business. It didn't seem right that he couldn't give her money. But that ship had sailed. Worse, he had to confess that he was the one who'd told her dad how well she was doing.

Wyatt looked at his watch, counting down the hours till naptime, feeling as if he was counting down the hours to doomsday.

CHAPTER SEVEN

STILL TOO WORKED UP to sit at a table and run numbers, Missy pulled a box of flour from her pantry, along with semisweet chocolate chips, sugar and cornstarch. Wyatt taking the kids without pushing for answers as to why she was so upset was about the nicest thing anyone had ever done for her, so she would repay him with a cake. A fancy chocolate cake with raspberry sauce.

While the cake baked, she took snacks and juice boxes out to the kids, with an extra for Wyatt. Though he accepted the cookies and juice box, he more or less stayed back, but she understood why. Not only had he seen her sobbing that morning, but she'd rejected his advances the night before. She didn't blame him for not wanting to talk to her.

But the cake would bring them back to their normal footing.

As it cooled, she put raspberry juice, cornstarch and a quarter cup of sugar into a saucepan. After it had boiled, she strained it to remove the seeds, then set it aside. Using more chocolate chips, she made the glaze for the cake.

By the time the kids returned to the house for lunch, the cake was ready. As usual, Wyatt didn't come inside with them. He went to his own house for lunch. But that was okay. While the kids napped, she'd take the baby monitor receiver with her and deliver the cake to him.

The kids washed up, ate lunch, brushed their teeth and crawled into their little beds.

Missy took a breath and tucked the monitor under her arm. She grabbed the cup of sauce in one hand and the cake in the other and carried the best looking cake she'd ever baked across her yard, under the shrub branch and to his porch.

She lightly kicked the door with her foot. "Wyatt?"

He appeared on the other side of the screen. "Yeah?"

She presented the cake. "I made this for you."

He glanced down at the cake, then back at

her. "I thought we talked about you baking me a cake?"

She laughed. "It's a thank-you for helping me out this morning. Not a thank-you for playing, because we both know that's wrong. It's thanks for helping me."

When he said nothing, she laughed again. "Open the door, idiot, so we can cut this thing and see if it tastes as good as it looks."

He opened the door and she stepped inside the modest kitchen. She set the cake on the table. "Where did your gram keep her knives?"

He walked to the cabinets, opened a drawer and retrieved a knife.

"Might as well get two forks and two plates while you're gathering things."

He silently did as he was told. She happily cut the cake. Dewy and moist, it sliced like a dream. She placed a piece on each plate, then drizzled raspberry sauce over them.

Handing one to Wyatt, she said, "There was supposed to be a whipped cream flower on each piece, but I didn't have enough hands to carry the whipped cream."

He sniffed a laugh, but didn't say anything.

That was when she felt the weirdness. Something was definitely up.

"The cake really is just a simple thank-you. No strings attached." She paused, pointing at his piece. "Try it."

He slid his fork into it and put a bite in his mouth. His eyes closed and he groaned. "Good God. That's heaven on a fork."

Pride tumbled through her. "I know! It's a simple recipe I found online. But it tastes like hours of slave labor."

She laughed again, but Wyatt set down his fork. "We have to talk."

At the stern tone of his voice, her appetite deserted her. She set her fork down, too. "You want to know what made me cry this morning."

He squeezed his eyes shut again, then popped them open. "Actually, that's the problem. I already know what made you cry this morning. When I was bringing the kids back after their surprise visit to my house, I overhead you and Monty."

"Oh." Embarrassment replaced pride. Heat slid up her cheeks. Her chest tightened.

"I heard him ask for money."

She said nothing, only stared at the pretty cake between them.

"I also heard what you said about him beating your mom, you and your sister."

She pressed her lips together.

"But that's not the worst of it."

Her head shot up and she caught his gaze. "Really? What can be worse than my dad beating me? About living a lie? About worrying every damn night that he was going to kill my mom, until she finally did die? What can be worse than that?"

"Look. I know it was a terrible thing."

"You know nothing." And she didn't want him to know anything. If she believed there was a chance for them to have a relationship, she might have told him. The timing was perfect. He already knew the overall story. She might have muddled through the humiliating details, if only because she was sick to death of living a lie. But knowing there was no chance for them, not even the possibility of love, she preferred to keep her secrets and her mortification to herself.

"I don't want to talk about it."

"Okay." His quiet acceptance tiptoed into

the room. From his tone she knew he wasn't happy with her answer, but he accepted it. "But I have to tell you one more thing." He dragged in another breath. "One day last week I ate at the diner. When I was done, I went back to the kitchen to say hello to your dad, and somehow the subject of you and your business came up—"

She jumped out of her seat. "Oh, my God! *You* told him?"

"I'm sorry."

She gaped at him, horrible things going through her brain. She'd spent years staying away from her dad, not going to town picnics and gatherings or anything even remotely fun to protect her kids. And in one casual conversation, Wyatt had ruined years of her sacrifice.

She grabbed the monitor and turned to leave.

"I'm sorry!"

She spun to face him. "He's a leech. A liar. A thief. I don't want him in my life! I especially don't want him around the kids!"

"Well, you know what?" Wyatt shot out of his chair and was in front of her before she could blink. "Then you should tell people that. Because normal people don't keep secrets from their dads. Which means other normal people don't suspect you're keeping a secret from yours."

Her chin rose. "I guess that means I'm not normal, then. Thanks for that." She pivoted and smacked her hands on his screen door, opening it. "I need to get back to the kids."

When she was gone, Wyatt fell to his chair. Part of him insisted he shouldn't feel bad. He hadn't known. She hadn't told him.

But he remembered his charmed childhood. He might not have been well liked at school, but he was well loved at home. What the hell did he know about being abused? What did he know about the dark reasons for keeping secrets?

He'd been born under a lucky star and he knew it.

He scrubbed his hands down his face. Looked over at the cake. It was the best thing he had ever tasted. Missy had talent. With a little help, she would succeed. Maybe even beyond her wildest dreams.

But like an idiot, he'd blocked his chance to help her, by offering her money so he could stop being attracted to her.

Her life was about so much more than sex and marriage and who was attracted to whom. It was about more than being praised and admired. All she wanted to do was make a living. Be safe. Keep her kids safe.

And Wyatt kept hurting her.

He was an idiot.

Missy spent the rest of the kids' nap in tears. Not because Wyatt had ratted her out to her dad. He couldn't have ratted her out. As he'd said, he hadn't known she kept her success a secret from her dad. Because she didn't tell anybody about him.

And if she really dug down into the reasons she was suddenly so sad, so weary of it all, that hit the top of the list.

She didn't talk to anybody. At least not beyond surface subjects. No one knew her. It was the coldest, emptiest, loneliest feeling in the world, to exist but not be known. In high school, she could pretend that the life she led during the day, in classes, at football games, cheering and being chosen to be homecoming queen, snowball queen and prom queen, was her real life.

But as she got older, her inability to have real friends, people she could talk to, wore on her. And when she really got honest with herself, she also had to admit that her company was a nice safe way of having to connect with people in only a superficial way. Once a wedding was over, she moved on to new people. No one ever stayed in her life.

Of course, she had wanted to connect with Wyatt, but he didn't want a relationship. He wanted a fling.

She swiped away her tears. It didn't matter. She was fine. When her dad was out of the picture, her life was good. And that morning she'd scared him off. He wouldn't be back. And if he did come back, testing to see if she was serious about her threats, she'd call the police. After a night or two in jail he would stay away for good. Because he was a coward.

Then the whole town would know and she'd be forced to deal with it. But at least her life wouldn't be a lie anymore.

And maybe she could come out from under this horrible veil of secrets that ended with nothing but loneliness.

When the kids awoke, she kept them inside, working on a special project with them: refrigerator art. She got out the construction paper, glue and little round-edged plastic scissors. They made green cats and purple dogs. Cut out yellow flowers and white houses. And glued everything on the construction paper, creating "art" she could hang for Nancy to see on Saturday when she babysat.

And outside, Wyatt sat on the bench seat of his gram's old wooden picnic table, peering through the openings in the tall shrubs, waiting for them to appear.

But the kids and Missy didn't come outside. Because she was angry? Or sad? Or in protection mode?

He didn't know.

All he knew was that it was his fault.

He rose from the picnic table and walked into his house, back to the bedroom littered with shoe boxes. He sat on the bed and began the task for looking for the jewelry, trying to get his mind off Missy.

It didn't work. He was about to give up, but had nothing else to do—damn his mother for canceling the cable. So he forced himself to open one more box, and discovered a stack of letters tied with a pink ribbon. He probably would have tossed them aside except for the unique return address.

It was a letter from his grandfather, Sergeant Bill McKenzie, to his grandmother, sent from Europe during World War II.

Wyatt sat on the bed, pulled the string of the bow.

Though his grandfather had died at least twenty years before, Wyatt remembered him as a tall, willowy guy who liked to tell jokes, and never missed a family event like a birthday party or graduation. He'd liked him. A lot. Some people even said Wyatt "took after" him.

He opened the first letter.

Dear Joni…
I hope this letter finds you well. Things here are quiet, for now. That's why I have time to write. I wanted to thank you and everyone at home for your efforts with the war bonds. I also know rationing is hard. I recognize what a struggle it is to do without and to work

in the factories. Tell everyone this means a great deal to those of us fighting.

The letter went on to talk about personal things, how much he missed her, how much he loved her, and Wyatt had to admit he got a bit choked up. A kid never thought of his grandparents loving each other. He'd certainly never pictured them young, fighting a war and sacrificing for a cause. But he could see his grandmother working in a factory, see his grandfather fighting for freedom.

What Wyatt hadn't expected to find, in letter after letter, was how much encouragement his grandfather had given his grandmother. Especially since, of the two, she was safer.

Still, his gram would have been a young woman. Working in a factory. Going without nylons—which might explain why she saved old panty hose. Getting up at the crack of dawn, doing backbreaking labor. He'd never thought of his grandparents this way, but now that he had, their lives and their love took on a new dimension for him.

Hours later, feeling hungry, he ambled to the

kitchen and saw the cake. He took a chunk of the half-eaten slice he'd left behind. Flavor exploded on his tongue like a recrimination.

He sat at the table, staring at the cake. His grandfather was such a people-smart guy that he never would have let anyone suffer in silence the way Missy was. Sure, she baked cakes and attended weddings, looking pretty and perky, as if everything was fine. But everything wasn't fine. She worked her butt off to support her kids, and probably lived her life praying her dad would forget she existed.

And Wyatt had blown that in a one-minute conversation after eating pie.

He had to do something to make that up to her. He had to do something to make her life better. He already watched her kids while she worked every morning, but from the way she'd kept them inside after their naps, she might be changing her mind about letting him do even that.

So that left her business. If he wanted to do something to help her, if he wanted to do something to make up for the things he'd done wrong, then he had to figure out how she could afford to hire an assistant and buy a van.

Without him giving her money.

The next morning, Missy got up, put on a pot of coffee, poured three bowls of cereal and three glasses of milk, and sat at the table.

"So what are you going to do today?"

Owen said, "Pway with Wyatt."

She stirred her coffee. "That sounds like a lot of fun, but he might not come over, so you should think about what you'd like to do with your sisters."

Lainie's head shot up and she gave her mom a wide-eyed look. Claire's little mouth fell open. For the past two weeks, they'd enjoyed a small heaven, playing dolls without being forced to also entertain their brother. Neither seemed happy to have that change.

A knock at the door interrupted them, turning Missy around to see who it was.

Wyatt opened the door. "I brought your cake plate and sauce cup back."

She rose, wiped her sweating palms down her

denim shorts. She took the plate and cup from him. "Thanks."

He smiled slightly. "Aren't you going to offer me a cup of coffee?"

Actually, she hoped he'd just go. Like Owen, she'd gotten accustomed to having someone to talk to, to be with. She hadn't even realized it until the night before, when she'd thought about how everybody came into her life, then left again. Even Wyatt would soon leave. But as they were jointly caring for her kids, and he helped her deliver her cakes, spending entire Saturdays with her, she'd been so preoccupied with her work that she'd been growing accustomed to having him around.

But he'd told her he didn't want to be in her life, and she had accepted that. She wished he'd just leave, so she could start her healing process.

Still, after years of working at the diner as a teenager, if someone asked for coffee, she poured it. "Sure. I have plenty of coffee."

He ambled to the table. "Hey, kids."

Lainie said, "Hi, Wyatt!"

Owen said, "Hey, Wyatt."

Claire smiled.

Owen said, "Are we going to pway?"

Wyatt pulled out a chair and sat. "As soon as I talk to your mom about some things." He pointed at the boy's bowl. "Are you done eating?"

Owen picked up his little plastic bowl and drank the contents in about ten seconds. Then he slapped the bowl on the table and grinned at Wyatt from behind a milk mustache.

Wyatt laughed. "Now you need to go wash up."

"You can all wash up, brush your teeth and head outside. Wyatt won't be far behind."

Missy knew that probably sounded rude. At the very least high-handed. But she'd made up her mind the night of the wedding. Even before he'd seen her dad at her door. If she got involved with him, she wanted something more. He didn't. Plus, in another day or week, he'd be gone. He wasn't really her friend, didn't want to be her lover, except temporarily. She had to break her attachment to him.

The kids scrambled along the short hall to their bathroom. She sat across from Wyatt.

"I'm not going to talk about my dad."

"That's not what I came to talk about."

"It isn't?"

"No. You know yesterday how I told you I was a thinker?"

"I thought you were just bragging."

He winced. "I was…sort of."

Her eyebrows rose, as if she was silently asking him what the hell that had to do with anything.

He squirmed uncomfortably. "The thing is, last night as I thought about your situation…"

"You can't help me. I have to handle my dad alone."

"I'm not talking about your dad. I'm talking about your business."

"And I thought we'd already been over this, too. I don't want your money."

"I'm not offering you money. I solve business problems all the time. And sitting there last night, I realized that if I'm such a hotshot, I should be able to solve yours, too."

She laughed. That hadn't occurred to her, but it was true. If he was such a hotshot he should be able to muddle through her measly little expansion problem. "Without offering me money."

"Right. We took that off the table the first week I was here."

"So. Now you're going to think about my problem?"

He picked up the saltshaker, turned it over in his hands as if studying it. "Actually, I solved it."

She snorted a laugh. "Right."

He finally caught her gaze. "I did. I don't know if you're going to be happy with the answer, but I took all the variables I knew into consideration, and realized that if I were in your position, I'd use the house as collateral for a line of credit."

She gasped. "Use my house?"

"I woke up my chief financial officer last night and had him run some numbers."

Wyatt pulled a paper from his back pocket. "He checked the value of your house against comps in the area, and estimates your house's value here." Wyatt pointed at the top number. "Which means you could easily get a hundred thousand dollar line of credit with the house as collateral."

She raised her gaze to his slowly. "But then I'd have a payment every month."

"You'd also have a van and an assistant, and you could take more weddings."

The truth of that hit her with a happy lift of her spirits. Though part of her struggled against it, her mind shifted into planning mode. "And maybe birthday cakes."

"And birthday cakes." He smiled sheepishly. "I ate that whole damned cake."

"Wyatt! That much sugar's not good for you."

"I know, but I'm out of food except for cereal, and I couldn't go to the diner."

Her face heated. "You can go wherever you want."

"I'll be damned if I'll give money to a guy who beat his family."

Owen came barreling into the kitchen. "Ready to pway?"

Wyatt pointed at the door. "You get everything set up outside. I'll be there in a minute." Owen raced out the door as Claire and Lainie appeared with their dolls.

"Are you going outside?"

They nodded.

Missy straightened the collar of Claire's shirt. "Okay. You know the rules. Stay in the yard."

They left and Wyatt caught her hand. "So? What do you think? Could you be okay with a line of credit?"

The warmth of his hand holding hers rendered her speechless for a few seconds, but she reminded herself he wasn't interested in her romantically, unless it was for an affair. What he was doing now was making up for talking about her to her dad.

Of course, that was sort of nice, too. If he didn't think of her as a friend, he'd blow off what he'd done. Instead, he was making it up to her. As a friend would.

She relaxed a bit. It wasn't wrong to take advice from a friend. Especially a friend who had business expertise. "It's a big step. I don't want to lose this house."

"Hey, who yelled at me for not having faith in you?"

"I did."

"Then have some faith in yourself. And diversify. I have a couple of people on staff who could look into markets for your cakes. Or you could just go to the grocery stores and restaurants in neighboring towns and offer them a cake or two.

Make the first week's free. When they see the reaction to them, they'll order."

Warmth spread through her. A feeling of normalcy returned. "You think I can do this?"

"Hell, yeah." Wyatt rose. "But it's more important that you know you can do it."

CHAPTER EIGHT

AT LUNCHTIME SHE FED the kids, wondering what Wyatt was eating. Then she saw him leave on his bike. She wouldn't let herself consider that he might be going to the diner. He'd said he wouldn't, but in her life people said a lot of things, then did the opposite. She just hoped he'd respect her enough not to say anything to her dad, not to warn him away or yell at him.

Twenty minutes later, when he returned with a bag from the grocery store, she relaxed. From the size of the bag, she knew he hadn't had enough time to shop as well as visit her dad. Maybe he really was a guy true to his word?

Falling into her normal daily routine, she straightened up the house while the kids napped. She picked up toys and vacuumed the living room and playroom floors. When she walked into the kitchen, she saw Wyatt at the door.

"How long have you been standing there?"

"Long enough to know you're a thorough vacuumer."

She laughed and opened the screen door. "Did you get lunch?"

"I stopped at the store for bread and deli meat. Do you know they don't have an in-house bakery anymore? They could use some homemade cakes in their baked goods section."

"You can stop spying for me. Once I get an assistant I'll investigate every store in the area."

"So you've decided to get the line of credit?"

"Yes. Using the house as collateral."

He walked to the table. "Can we sit?"

"Why? Are you going to help me call the bank?"

He pulled some papers from his back pocket. "Actually, I'd like to be the bank."

She gasped. "I told you I don't want your money."

"And I told you that I feel responsible for the mess with your dad yesterday. This is my way of making that up to you." He caught her gaze. "Besides, I'm going to give you a point and a half below the current interest rate at the bank, and my people have worked out a very flexible repayment schedule. No matter what happens with your business, you will not lose this house."

Her heart tripped over itself in her chest. *She wouldn't lose her house?* She didn't know a bank that promised that. And Wyatt hadn't gone to the diner. He'd bought deli meat. Even though she knew he was growing tired of not eating well, he'd been true to his word.

"And it's a loan?"

He handed the papers to her. "Read the agreement. Though I promise not to take the house if you default, a new payment schedule will be created. But if you sell the house, you have to pay me the balance of the loan with the proceeds. No matter what happens, you have to pay back the hundred grand." He pointed to a paragraph at the bottom of page one. "And you have to take out a life insurance policy in the amount of a hundred thousand dollars with me as beneficiary, if you die."

Hope filled her. He hadn't merely stayed away from her dad; he'd listened to everything she'd been saying the past few weeks. "So it really is a business deal?"

"Albeit with very good terms for you. I know

you don't want any special favors, but even you have to admit I owe you."

She licked her lips. Lots of people had done her wrong, but no one had ever even acknowledged that, let alone tried to make up for it.

"You can take that to an attorney, if you want."

She smiled up at him. "I could take it to my former boss at the law firm."

Wyatt rose. "Smart businesswoman that you are, I would expect no less from you."

That night, Wyatt sat on the big wicker chair on his back porch, once again wishing his mom hadn't canceled the cable. He'd dug through more boxes, read a few more of his grandfather's letters and still wasn't tired enough for bed. Leaning back in the big chair, he closed his eyes.

"Hey, are you asleep?"

He bounced up with a short laugh. Missy stood at the bottom of his porch steps, holding two bottles of beer and the papers he'd given her that afternoon.

"I guess I was."

She waved the papers. "Can I come up?"

He rose. "Sure. Your lawyer's already looked at those?"

She wore a pink top and white shorts, and had the front of her hair tied back in some sort of clip contraption, but her smile was what caught him. Bright and radiant as the closest star, it raised his hopes and eased his guilt.

She handed him a beer. "To celebrate. My old boss squeezed me in, read the papers in about ten minutes and told me I'd be a fool not to sign." She clanked her beer bottle against Wyatt's. "He's read your comics, by the way. He called you a genius."

Wyatt scuffed his tennis shoe on the old gray porch planks. "I don't know about genius."

"Oh, don't go getting all modest on me now."

He laughed. "So you're signing?"

She handed the papers to him. "It's already signed and notarized. My lawyer kept a copy and made a copy for me."

Wyatt took the papers, glanced down at her signature. "Good girl." Then he clanked his bottle to hers again. "Congratulations. Someday you're going to be the superstar this town talks about."

She fell into one of the big wicker chairs. "This town doesn't care about superstars. We're all about making ends meet."

He sat, too. It was the first time since he'd been home that she'd been totally relaxed with him. He took a swig of his beer, then said, "There's no shame in that."

"I think about ninety percent of America lives that way."

The conversation died and he really wished it hadn't. There was a peace about her, a calmness that he'd never seen before.

"So you're happy?"

"I'm ecstatic. Within the next month I'll have a van, an assistant and day care for the kids." She turned to him. "Do you know how good it is for kids to socialize?"

He didn't. Not really. He knew very little about kids. What he knew was business and comics. So he shrugged. "I guess pretty important."

"Owen will have other boys to play with."

Though Wyatt got a stab of jealousy over that, he also knew he was leaving soon. With or without the jewelry, he couldn't stay away from his work more than a month, five weeks tops.

"That can't be anything but good."

Another silence fell between them. After a few minutes she turned to face him. "I don't know how to deal with someone who knows about my dad."

"Really?"

"Yeah. I've been keeping the secret so long it feels odd that another person knows. It's almost like who I am around you is different."

He laughed. "That's funny, because I've been thinking the same thing since I came here."

"That I'm different?"

"No. More that I can't get my footing. In Florida I'm king of my company. Here, I know nothing about kids or cakes or weddings. Plus, I'm the guy you remember as a nerd."

"You're so not a nerd."

"Geek then."

She shook her head. "Have you looked at yourself in the mirror lately?"

He glanced down at his jeans, then back at her. "I wore jeans in high school."

"Yeah. But not so well."

He laughed.

She smiled. "It's like you're the first person in my life to know the whole me. Past and present."

"And you're the first person to know the whole me. Geek and sex god."

She laughed and rose from her seat. "Right." Reaching for his empty beer bottle, she said, "Before that little display of conceit, I was going to ask if you wanted to help me van shop."

"I'd *love* to help you van shop."

"See? Old Wyatt wouldn't have been able to do that."

"Old Wyatt?"

"The geeky high school kid."

"Right."

"But older, wiser Wyatt can."

He chuckled. No one ever called him old, let alone wise. But he sort of liked it. Just as she had her fortes with kids and cakes, he had his expertise, too. "So you're going to let me go with you?"

"Yes." She turned and started down the stairs. "And don't go getting any big ideas about buying some tricked out supervan. I saw the clause in the agreement where you can raise the amount of the loan to accommodate expansion. I don't want any more money. I have to grow the business in stages. We get a normal van. I hire a normal assistant. The kids go to local day care."

By the time she finished she was at the bottom of the steps. She turned to face him.

He saluted her. "Aye, aye, Captain."

She laughed. "I also like your new sense of humor. Young Wyatt didn't laugh much."

He leaned on the porch railing. Since they were being honest, it was time to admit the truth. "He was always too busy being nervous. Especially around you. You're so beautiful you probably make most men nervous."

She shook her head as if she thought he was teasing, then pointed at the hedge. "I've gotta go. See you tomorrow."

"See you tomorrow."

He pushed away from the railing, smiling to himself. She was correct. He felt odd around her because she was the first, maybe the only person in his life to know both sides of him.

But now he also knew her secret. Instead of that scaring him the way he knew it probably should, because her secret was dark and frightening and needed to be handled with care, he

felt a swell of pride. She hadn't told him her secret, but she clearly trusted him with it. He felt
honored.

"Hi, Mommy."

Missy opened her eyes and smiled down at the
foot of the bed. Claire grinned at her. She never
awoke after the kids. She couldn't imagine why
she'd slept so late. Except that being honest with
Wyatt about her dad, and accepting the loan,
had relaxed her. She didn't have to pretend that
everything was fine around him. She could be
herself.

"Hey, sweetie. Want some cereal?"

Her daughter's grin grew and she nodded.

Missy rolled out of bed. Normally she was
already in shorts and a T-shirt before she went
to the kitchen. Today she was so far behind she
didn't have time to change. Still, she slept in pajama pants and a tank top. There was no reason
to change or even to find a robe. She sleepily
padded from her bedroom in the back corner
of the downstairs into the kitchen. As she got
cereal from the cupboard and Claire climbed

onto a chair, Lainie and Owen ambled into the kitchen. They also climbed onto chairs.

She'd barely gotten cocoa chunks cereal into three bowls and a pot of coffee on before there was a knock at her door. Without waiting for her to invite him in, Wyatt entered.

"Are you here to mooch coffee?"

He laughed. "No, but I wouldn't say no if you'd offer me a cup."

She motioned for him to take a seat at the table, grabbed a cup from the cupboard and poured some coffee into it for him.

When she set it in front of him, his gaze touched on her tank top, then rippled down to her pajama pants. "I guess I'm early for the van shopping."

She stifled the warmth and pleasure that saturated her at his obvious interest. Saturday they'd decided against any kind of relationship because they wanted two different things. Yesterday, when she'd signed the line of credit papers, they'd cemented that. Even if he wanted to get involved with her—which he didn't—she wouldn't get involved with a man who owned the "mortgage" on her house.

"You want to go today?"

"No time like the present. My bank wire transferred the hundred grand into a new account set up for you. We can stop at the bank for you to sign the paperwork, and the money will be at your disposal immediately."

Her attraction to him was quickly forgotten as her heart filled with joy. This was really happening. She was getting a van, a helper... She would expand her business!

"Let me call Nancy to babysit." Missy popped out of her chair and raced back to the bedroom to get her phone. After Nancy agreed to come over, she hopped into the shower. Halfway done shampooing her hair, she realized she'd left the kids with Wyatt. Without thinking.

She trusted him.

She ducked her hair under the spray. She did trust him.

She waited for her tummy to twist or her breathing to become painful at the thought of trusting someone so easily, so completely, that she didn't even think to ask him to mind the kids, but nothing happened.

She finished her shower, fixed her hair and slid

into jeans and a blue T-shirt. In a way she was glad they'd decided on Saturday night against a relationship, because her feelings for him had nothing to do with her attraction—or his. The trust she felt for him was simple, honest. Just as she'd realized his lending her money was like something a friend would do to make up for a wrong, her leaving her kids without thought was also the act of a friend.

They were becoming *friends.*

Tucking her hair behind her ears, she walked into the kitchen to find Wyatt filling the sink with soapy water as her children brought their cereal bowls to him.

"How'd you get them to do that?"

"Bribery."

Her mouth fell open. "Wyatt—"

"Relax. I promised them another trip to my grandmother's house to look through boxes. Nothing sinister like ice cream."

She casually walked to the table. "Ice cream isn't a bad idea."

He turned from the sink. "It isn't?"

"No. There's a nice place a mile or so out of town." She peeked at him, testing this friendship they were forming. Though her stomach jumped a bit at how handsome he was, she reminded herself that was normal. "Maybe we could take the kids there when I get the van. You know? Use getting ice cream as a maiden voyage."

He appeared surprised. "Sounds great."

Nancy knocked on the door and walked into the kitchen. "I heard there's a bunch of kids here who want to play house with me."

The girls jumped for joy. "Yay!"

But Owen deflated.

Wyatt stooped down to talk to him. "Don't worry. Van shopping won't take all day. And when we get back you can do whatever you want."

"Wook for tweasure?"

"Sure."

Missy's heart swelled. If they hadn't had the talk about their relationship she'd be in serious danger of falling in love with this guy. But they had had the talk. Then he'd overheard her argument with her father. And now they were friends.

Outside, she rummaged through her purse for her SUV keys. But when she reached the driver's side door, she noticed he hadn't followed.

"Aren't you sick of that beast yet?"

She laughed. "What?"

He jangled his keys. "It's such a beautiful day. Let's take the bike."

Happiness bubbled in her veins. "I haven't been on a bike since high school."

He grabbed the thin shrub branch and pushed it aside for her. "Then it's time."

With a laugh, she dipped under and walked over to the garage door. He opened it and there sat his shiny black bike.

"I don't have a helmet."

"You can use mine."

He handed her the helmet and straddled the bike.

She licked her suddenly dry lips. For all her fancy, happy self-talk that morning about being glad they were becoming friends, the thought of straddling the bike behind him sent shivers up her spine.

She'd danced with him. She'd kissed him. She knew the potency of his nearness.

And in spite of all that happy self-talk, she was susceptible. He was good to her. He was good to her kids. And around him she felt like a woman. Not just a mom.

She liked that feeling as much as she liked the idea of being his friend.

"Come on! Don't be a chicken."

Glad that he mistook her hesitancy for fear, she sucked in a breath. She could stop this just by saying she'd changed her mind and wanted to take the SUV. But then she'd miss the chance to hold him without worry he'd get the wrong impression. The chance to slide her cheek against his back. The chance to inhale his scent.

And the chance to enjoy him for a few minutes without consequences. Because, God help her, she did like him as more than a friend. He was the one who didn't want her. And if she refused this chance to be close to him, she'd regret it.

She slid onto the bike.

He revved the engine as she plopped the helmet on her head. Within seconds they shot out of the garage and onto the quiet street. She wrapped her arms around his middle, not out of a desire to hold him, but out of sheer terror.

Then the wind caught her loose hair beneath the helmet and whooshed along her limbs. Gloriously free, she raised her arms, let them catch the breeze and yelled, "Woo hoo!"

She felt rather than heard him laugh. In under five minutes, they were at the bank. She pulled off the helmet and he wrapped the straps around the handlebars before they walked into the lobby.

The customer service representative quickly found her file. Missy signed papers. Wyatt signed papers. And within what seemed like seconds they were on the bike again.

He pulled out onto Main Street and stopped at the intersection. He turned his head and yelled, "What car dealer do you want to go to?"

"I thought you'd know."

"I haven't been around here for a while." He revved the bike and smiled at her. His dark eyes shone with devilishness that called to her. "We could just get on the highway and drive until we find something."

Part of her wanted to. The kids were cared for. She was in a wonderful, daring mood. And he was so close. So sweet. So full of mischief…

Mischief with someone she really liked was dangerous to a mother of three who was knee-deep in a fledgling business. She pulled out her phone. "Or I could look up dealers online."

"Spoilsport." He revved the bike. "I like my idea better." He shot out into the street again. They flew down Main Street and again she had to stifle the urge to put her hands in the air and yell, "Woo hoo!"

But she stifled it. Because as much fun as this was, she had to get a van and get home to her kids.

A little voice inside her head disagreed. She didn't need to get home. Nancy was at the house. The kids were fine. And Missy was out. Out of the house. On her way to buy a van. On her way to having a wonderful future because her business would succeed. She knew it would.

Then she remembered the look of mischief in Wyatt's eyes. That was why she needed to get home. She liked him. Really liked him. And he wanted an affair. That was a bad combo. She hit a few buttons on her phone and began looking for a used car dealer.

Wyatt got them on the highway. The bike's speed picked up. Wind rushed at her. The sun warmed her arms. She put her face up and inhaled.

"Find a place yet?"

When Wyatt's voice whispered in her ear, she almost flew off the bike. He chuckled. "I turned on the mic." He showed her the mouthpiece hanging from the phone piece in his ear.

She said, "Oh." She shouldn't have been surprised by the communications equipment. In his real world, Wyatt probably had every gadget known to mankind. After a few flips through the results of her internet search on her phone screen, she said, "There's a place right off the highway about a mile down the road."

"Then that's where we'll go."

They drove the mile, took the exit ramp and stopped in the parking lot of a car dealer. Shiny new cars, SUVs, trucks and vans greeted them.

She slid off the bike. "Wow. There are so many cars here."

Wyatt smoothed his hand along the fender of a brand-new red truck. "Too bad you need a van." He whistled as he walked along the back panels. "Look at this thing."

She laughed. "You should buy it for yourself."

He lovingly caressed some chrome. "I should." He turned toward the big building behind the rows and rows of vehicles. "I think I'll just go find a salesman."

He came back ten minutes later with a salesman who first told him all the finer points of the brand-new red truck, then turned to her as Wyatt climbed into the truck cab.

"I hear you need a van."

She smiled slightly. "Yes."

"Do you know what you want?"

"Yes. A white one."

He laughed. "No. I was talking about engine size, cargo bay versus seating."

Wyatt jumped out of the truck. "She wants a V-8, with seats that retract so that she has enough space to deliver goods."

"What kind of goods? How much space?"

"She bakes wedding cakes. The space doesn't need to be huge. We just need to know that the van can be easily air-conditioned."

"Are you sure she doesn't want to order a refrigerated van?"

Missy opened her mouth to speak, but Wyatt

said, "She's on a limited budget. She doesn't need to go overboard."

They looked at several vans. Test drove three. In the end, she bought a white van that was used rather than new. She didn't know anything about refrigerated vans, but it sounded like something she might need in the future. Given that the used van was twelve thousand dollars less than a new one, she wouldn't be wasting as much if she decided a year or two from now to get the refrigerated van. Exclusively for business. She might even be able to keep the used van for her kids.

She suddenly felt like a princess—buying what she needed, planning to buy something even better in the future.

They walked into the office to write up the papers for her van. She called the bank and made arrangements to do a wire transfer of the purchase price, then signed on the dotted line.

The salesman stapled her papers together and gave her a set. "Okay. Van will be delivered tomorrow morning."

He then passed a bunch of papers to Wyatt. "And for the truck."

He said, "Thanks," and signed a few things.

The salesman handed him the keys. "Pleasure doing business with you, Mr. McKenzie. You know, if you get tired of the red one, I also have it in blue and yellow."

Wyatt laughed.

It was then that it hit her how rich he was. Sure, she'd always known in an abstract way that he had money. But watching him see something he wanted and buy it without a moment's hesitation or a single second thought made it real. This guy she liked, someone who was a friend, had more money than she could even imagine.

They walked out into the bright sunshine. He slid onto the bike. She put the helmet on her head and got on behind him. As he started off, she slid her arms around his waist and squeezed her eyes shut. He was so far out of her league. So different than anybody she knew.

Sadness made her sigh. Still, she leaned in close to him. Because he couldn't see her, she let her eyes drift shut, and enjoyed the sensation of just holding him. Because he was tempting. Because she was grateful. Because for once in her life, she really, really wanted somebody, but she was smart enough to know she couldn't have him.

And if she didn't take this chance to hold him, to feel the solidness of him beneath her chest, she might not ever get another.

When they returned to his gram's, she removed the helmet. He looped the strap over the handlebars.

"So? Fun?"

She refused to let her sadness show and spoil their day. "Oh, man. So much fun. I loved the bike ride, but I loved buying the van even more. I've never been able to get what I wanted. I've always had to take what I could afford."

He grinned. "It's a high, isn't it?"

"Yeah, but I'm not going to let myself get too used to it. For me, it's all part of getting my business up and running."

He nodded. "So, go feed the kids lunch and I'll be over around two to play with Owen."

She said, "Okay," and turned to go, but then faced Wyatt again. He was great. Honest. Open. Generous. And she'd always had her guard up around him. But now he knew her secret. He knew the real her. And he still treated her wonderfully.

She walked over and stood on her tiptoes. Intending to give him a peck on his check, in the last second she changed her mind. When her toes had her tall enough to reach his face, she kissed his lips. One soft, quick brush of her mouth across his that was enough to send electricity to her toes.

"Thanks."

He laughed. "I'd say you're welcome, but you owed me that kiss."

"I did?"

"If you'd kept our date graduation night, you'd have kissed me."

"Oh, really?"

"I might have been a geek, but that night I knew what I wanted and I was getting it."

She laughed, but stopped suddenly.

"What?"

She shook her head, turned away. "It's nothing."

He caught her hand and hauled her back. "It's something."

She stared at the front of his T-shirt. "The first

day you arrived, I wanted to say I was sorry I broke that date." She swallowed. "I was all dressed to go, on my way to the door…" She looked up. "But my dad hit my mom. Bloodied her lip."

Wyatt cursed. "You don't have to tell me this."

"Actually, I want to. I think it's time to let some of this out." She held his gaze. "I trust you."

"Then why don't we go into the house and you can tell me the whole story?"

She almost told him she should get back to the kids, but her need to rid herself of the full burden of this secret told her to take a few minutes, be honest, let some of this go.

She nodded and they walked to the back door of his grandmother's house and into her kitchen. He made a pot of coffee, then leaned against the counter.

"Okay…so what happened that night?"

"We'd had a halfway decent graduation. It was one of those times when Dad had to be on his best behavior because we were in public, so everything went well. I actually felt normal. But driving home, he stopped at a bar. When he got home, he freaked out. He'd been on good behavior so long he couldn't keep up the pretense anymore and he exploded. He slammed the kitchen door, pivoted and hit my mom. Her lip was bleeding, so I took her to the sink to wash it off and get ice, and he just turned and punched Althea, slamming her into the wall." Missy squeezed her eyes shut, remembering. "It was a nightmare, but then again lots of times were like that."

"Scary?"

She caught his gaze. "More than scary. Out of control. Like playing a game where the rules constantly change. What made him happy one day could make him angry the next. But even worse was the confusion."

"Confusion worse than changing rules?"

She swallowed. "Emotional, personal confusion."

Wyatt said nothing. She sucked in a breath. "Imagine what it feels like to be a little girl who wants nothing but to protect her mom, so you step in front of a punch."

He cursed.

"From that point on, I became fair game to him."

"He began to beat you, too?"

She nodded. "It was like I'd given him permission when I stepped into the first punch." She licked her lips. "So from that point on, my choice became watch him beat my mom, or take some of the beating for her."

Wyatt's eyes squeezed shut, as if he shared her misery through imagining it. "And you frequently chose to be beaten."

"Sometimes I had to."

She walked to the stove, ran her finger along the shiny rim. "But that night he couldn't reach me. I'd taken my mother to the sink, stupidly believing that without anyone to hit, he'd get frustrated and head for the sofa. But he went after Althea."

"How old was she?"

"Twelve. Too young to take full-fist beating from a grown man."

"I'm sorry."

Missy sucked in another breath. Hearing the truth coming from her own mouth, her anger at herself, disappointment in herself, and the grief she felt over losing Althea began to crumble. She'd been young, too. Too young to take the blame for things her father had done.

She loosened her shoulders, faced Wyatt again. "I could see her arm was broken, so I didn't think. I didn't speak. I didn't ask permission or wait for instructions. I just grabbed the car keys to take her to the hospital, and my dad yanked the bottle of bleach off the washer by the back door." Missy looked into Wyatt's dark, solemn eyes. "He took off the cap and, two seconds before I would have been out of range, tossed it at me. It ran down my skirt, washing out the color, eating holes right through the thin material."

Wyatt shook his head. "He was insane."

"I'd earned that dress myself." Her voice wobbled, so she paused long enough to strengthen it. She was done being a victim, done being haunted by her dad. It appeared even her ghosts of guilt over Althea leaving were being exorcized. "I worked for every penny I'd needed to buy it. But when he was drunk, he forgot things like that. As I was scrambling out of the dress, before the bleach burned through to my skin, he called me a bunch of names. I just tossed the dress in the trash and walked to my room. I put on jeans and a T-shirt and took Althea to the hospital. His screams and cursing followed us out the door and to the car."

Wyatt said nothing.

She stayed quiet for a few seconds, too, letting it soak in that she'd finally told someone, and that in telling someone she'd seen that she wasn't to blame. That she had no sin. No part in any of it except victim. And she was strong enough now not to accept that title anymore.

"At the hospital, a social worker came into the cubicle. Althea wanted to tell, to report our dad. I wouldn't let her." Missy glanced up at him again. "I feared for Mom. I knew the social worker would take us away, but Mom would be stuck there. And because we'd embarrassed him, he'd be even worse to her than he already was."

"Why didn't your mom leave?"

"She was afraid. She had no money. No skills. And he really only beat her about twice a month."

Wyatt sniffed in derision. "He's a bastard."

"I left the next day. Got a clerical job in D.C. and an apartment with some friends. Althea spent every weekend with us. I guess that was enough for my dad to realize we didn't need him—didn't depend on him—and we could report him, because he stopped hitting Mom. When Althea graduated, she left town. Went to college in California. We haven't really heard from her since." Saying that aloud hurt. Missy loved and missed her sister. But she wasn't the reason Althea had gone. She could let go of that now. "When one of my roommates moved out, I tried to get my mom to move in with me, but she refused. A few weeks later she had a heart attack and died."

Wyatt gaped at her. "How old was she?"

"Not quite fifty. But she was worn down, anorexic. She never ate. She was always too worried to eat. It finally killed her."

With her story out, exhaustion set in. Missy's shoulders slumped.

He turned to the coffeepot, poured two cups. "Here."

She smiled shakily. "That wasn't so bad."

"Secrets are always better if you tell them."

She laughed. "How do you know?"

He shrugged. "School, I guess. In grade school I hid the fact that I was bullied from my parents. But in high school I knew I couldn't let it go on. The kids were bigger, meaner, and I was no match. So I told them. They talked to the school principal. At first the bullies kept at me, but after enough detention hours, and seeing that I wasn't going to be their personal punching bag anymore, they stopped."

Missy laughed, set her cup on the counter beside him and flattened her hands on his chest. "Poor baby."

"I'd have paid good money to have you tell me that in high school."

"I really did like you, you know. I thought of you as smart and honest."

"I was."

She peeked up at him. "You are now, too."

The room got quiet. They stood as close as lovers, but something more hummed between them. Emotionally, she'd never been as connected to anyone as she was to him right now. She knew he didn't want anything permanent, but in this minute, she didn't, either. All she wanted was the quiet confirmation that, secrets shared, she would feel in the circle of his arms. She wanted to feel. To be real. To be whole.

Then she heard the kids out in the yard. Her kids. Her life. She didn't need sex to tell her she was real, whole. She had a life. A good life. A life she'd made herself. She had a cake to bake this Saturday. Soon she'd have an assistant. She'd make cakes for grocery stores and restaurants. Her life had turned out better than she'd expected. She had good things, kids to live for, a business that made her happy.

She stepped away. A one-night stand would be fun. But building a good life was better. "I've gotta go."

He studied her. "You're okay?"

"I'm really okay." She smiled. "I'm better than okay. Thanks for letting me talk to you."

"That's what friends do."

Her smile grew. The tension in her chest eased. "Exactly. So if you have any deep, dark secrets, I'm here for you, friend."

"You know my story. Stood up to bullies in high school, made lots of money, bad marriage, worse divorce—which I'm beginning to feel better about, thank you for asking."

She laughed and headed for the door. "Well, if you ever need to talk, you know where I am."

"Like I said, I have no secrets."

She stopped, faced him again. He might not have secrets, but he did have hurts. Hurts he didn't share.

Were it not for those hurts, she probably wouldn't push open the door and walk away. She'd probably be in his arms right now. But she did push on the screen door, did leave his kitchen. They were both too smart to get involved when he couldn't let go of his past.

CHAPTER NINE

SATURDAY MORNING Wyatt didn't wait until Missy was ready to leave to get dressed to help deliver her cake. She hadn't yet hired an assistant. She'd put an ad in the papers for the nearby cities, and a few responses had trickled in. But she wasn't about to jump into anything. She wanted time for interviews and to check references.

He couldn't argue with that. Which meant he'd need to help her with that week's wedding.

So Friday he'd bought new clothes, telling himself he was tired of looking like a grunge rocker. Saturday morning, after his shower, he had black trousers, a white shirt and black-and-white print tie to put on before he ambled to her house. As had become his practice, he knocked twice and walked in.

Then stopped.

Wearing an orange-and-white-flowered strapless sundress, and with her hair done up in a fancy do that let curls fall along the back of her neck, she absolutely stopped his heart. In a bigger city, she would have been the "it" girl. In a little town like Newland, with nowhere to go but the grocery store or diner, and no reason to dress up, she sort of disappeared.

"You look amazing." He couldn't help it; the words tumbled out of their own volition.

She smiled sheepishly. "Would you believe this is an old work dress? Without the little white jacket, it's perfect for a garden wedding."

He looked her up and down once again, his heart pitter-pattering. "I should get a job at that law firm if everyone looks that good."

Because he'd flustered her, and was having a bit of trouble keeping his eyes off her, he searched for a change of subject. Glancing around her kitchen, he noticed the five layers of cake sitting in a row on her counter. Oddly shaped and with what looked to be steel beams trimming the edges, it wasn't her most attractive creation.

"Is the bride a construction worker?"

"That's the Eiffel Tower." Missy laughed. "The groom proposed there."

"Oh." Wyatt took a closer look. "Interesting."

"It is to them."

Owen skipped into the room. "Hey, Wyatt."

"Hey, kid." He faced Missy, asking, "When's Nancy get here?" But his heart sped up again just from looking at her. She had the kind of legs that were made to be shown off, and the dress handled that nicely. Nipped in at the waist, it also accented her taut middle. The dip of the bodice showed just enough cleavage to make his mouth water.

And he thought *he* looked nice. She put him and his white shirt and black trousers to shame—even with a tie.

"She should be here in about ten minutes. If you help me load up, we can get on the road as soon as she arrives."

Making several trips, Missy and Wyatt put the layers of cake into the back of her new van. Together they carried the bottom layer, which had little people and trees painted on the side, mimicking street level around Paris's most famous landmark.

"Cute."

"It is cute. To the bride and groom." She grinned. "And it's banana walnut with almond filling."

He groaned. "I'll bet that's delicious."

Sixteen-year-old Nancy walked up the drive. Her dark hair had been pulled into a ponytail. In a pair of shorts and oversize T-shirt, she was obviously ready to play.

"Hi, Missy. Wyatt."

The kids came barreling out. She scooped them into her arms. "What first? Cartoons or sandbox?"

Owen said, "Sandbox."

The girls whined. But Nancy held her ground. "Owen has to get the chance to pick every once in a while."

After a flurry of goodbyes and a minute for Missy to find her purse, she and Wyatt boarded the van. He glanced around with approval. "So much better than the SUV."

"I know."

She started the engine and pulled out of the driveway onto the street. In a few minutes they were on the highway.

She peeked over at him. "So…you look different. Very handsome."

Her compliment caused his chest to swell with pride. He'd had hundreds of women come on to him since he'd become rich, but none of their compliments affected him as Missy's did. But that was wrong. They'd decided to be friends.

Pretending to be unaffected, he flipped his tie up and let it fall. "You know, I don't even dress like this for my own job."

"That's because you're the boss. Here I'm the boss."

"You never told me you wanted me to dress better."

"I think it was implied by the way everybody around you dressed. It's called positive peer pressure."

He chuckled, then sneaked a peek at her. Man. He'd never seen anybody prettier. Or happier. And what made it even better was knowing he'd played a part in her happiness. She wanted this business to succeed and it would. Because she'd let him help.

Pride shimmied through him, but so did his darned attraction again, stronger and more potent than it had been before she complimented him. But they'd already figured out they wanted two different things. The night before, she'd even offered to listen to his troubles. Smart enough not to want to get involved with him, she'd offered them the safe haven of friendship. He shouldn't be thinking of her any way, except as a friend.

It took two hours to get to the country club where the reception was being held. The party room of the clubhouse had been decorated in green and ivory, colors that flowed out onto the huge deck. The banister swirled with green and ivory tulle, down stairs that led guests to a covered patio where tables and chairs had been arranged around two large buffet tables.

As they carried the cake into the clubhouse, Missy said, "Wedding was at noon. Lunch will be served around one-thirty. Cake right after that, then we're home."

He snorted. "After a two-hour drive."

"Now, don't be huffy. Because we get home early, I'm making dinner and insisting you eat with us."

"You are?"

"Yep. And I'm not even cooking something on the grill. I'm making real dinner."

"Oh, sweetheart. You just said the magic words. *Real dinner.* You have no idea how hungry I am."

She laughed. They put the cake together on a table set up in a cool, shaded section of the room. When the wedding guests arrived, however, no one came into the building or even climbed up to the deck. Instead, they gathered on the patio, choosing their lunch seats, getting drinks from the makeshift bar.

The bride and groom followed suit. On the sunny, beautiful May day, no one went any farther than the patio.

"One of two things has to happen here," Missy said as she looked out the window onto the guests who were a floor below them. "Either we need to get people in here or we need to get the cake out there."

He headed for the door. "I'll go talk to somebody."

She put her hand on his forearm to stop him. "*I'll* go talk to somebody."

She walked through the echoing room and

onto the equally empty deck, down the stairs to the covered patio. Wyatt watched her look through the crowd and finally catch the attention of a tuxedo-clad guy.

She smiled at him and began talking. Even from a distance Wyatt saw the sparkle in her eyes, and his gaze narrowed in on the guy she was talking to. Tall, broad-shouldered, with dark curly hair, he wasn't bad looking… Oh, all right, he was good-looking, and was wearing a tux. Wyatt knew how women were about men in tuxes. He'd taken advantage of that a time or two himself. And Missy was a normal woman. A woman he'd rejected. She had every right to be attracted to this guy.

Even if it did make Wyatt want to punch something.

As she and the man in the tux walked up the stairs to the deck, he scrambled away from the window. She opened the door and motioned around the empty room.

"See? No one's even come in here."

The man in the tux glanced around, his gaze finally alighting on her creation. "Is that the cake?"

She smiled. "Yes."

Tux man strolled over. He examined the icing-covered Eiffel Tower, then looked over his shoulder at Missy, who had followed him. "You're remarkable."

Her cheeks pinkened prettily. Wyatt's eyes narrowed again.

"I wouldn't say remarkable." She grinned at him. "But I am good at what I do."

"And beautiful, too."

Unable to stop himself, Wyatt headed for the cake table.

Missy's already pink cheeks reddened. "Thanks. But as you can see, the cake—"

"I don't suppose you'd give a beleaguered best man your phone number?"

Her eyes widened. Wyatt's did, too. Beleaguered best man? Did he think he was in a Rodgers and Hammerstein play?

"I—"

He slid his hand into his pocket. "I have a pen."

Wyatt finally reached them. "She's got a pen, too, bud. If she wanted to give you her phone number, she could. But it seems she doesn't want to."

Missy shot Wyatt a stay-out-of-this look, then smiled politely at the best man. "What my assistant is trying to say is that I'm a very busy person. I keep a pen and paper for brides-to-be, who see my cakes and want to talk about me baking for them."

The best man stiffened. "So you wanting to get the cake downstairs, into the crowd, is all about PR for you?"

"Heavens, no." She laughed airily. "I want the bride to see the cake she designed."

But the best man snorted as if he didn't believe her. He shoved his hands into his pockets, casually, as if he held all the cards and knew it. "I guess you'll just have to figure out a way to get the bride up here yourself, then."

But Missy didn't bite. She smiled professionally and said, "Okay." Not missing a beat, she walked over to the French doors leading to the deck and went in search of the bride.

His threat ignored, the best man deflated and headed for the door, too.

Wyatt chuckled to himself. She certainly was focused. The best man might have temporarily knocked her off her game, but she'd quickly rebounded.

A few minutes later, Missy returned to the room in the clubhouse, the bride and groom on her heels.

"As you can see, nobody's here."

The bride stopped dead in her tracks. "That's my cake?"

Missy pressed her hand to her throat. "You said you wanted the Eiffel tower."

The bride slowly walked over. She ambled around the table, examining the cake. Wyatt stifled the urge to pull his collar away from his neck. In the quiet, empty room, the click of the bride's heels as she rounded the table was the only sound. Her face red, Missy watched helplessly.

Finally the bride said, "It's beautiful. So real. Isn't it, Tony?"

Tony said, "Yeah. It's cool. I like it."

"I think I'll have the band announce that we're cutting the cake up here, and ask everyone to join us."

Missy sighed with relief. "Sounds good."

Tony caught the bride's hand and they went back to the patio.

As soon as they were gone, Missy turned on Wyatt. "And *you.*"

"Me?" This time he did run his fingers under his shirt collar to release the strangled feeling. "What did I do?"

She stalked over to him. In her pretty orange-and-white-flowered dress and her tall white sandals, with her hair all done up, she looked like a Southern belle on the warpath.

"I fight my own battles. He was a jerk, but I handled him. Professionally. Politely."

"He was a letch."

She tossed her hands in the air. "I've handled letches before. Sheesh! Do you think he's the first best man to come on to me?"

Wyatt's blood froze, then heated to boiling and roared through his veins. "Best men come on to you?"

"And ushers and fathers of the bride—or groom." She stepped into his personal space. "But I'm a big girl. I can handle myself with bad boys."

He snorted. "Oh, really?"

"You think I can't?"

His hands slipped around the back of her neck, pulling her face to his as he lowered his head. His lips met hers in a flurry of passion and desire. He expected her to back off, to be stunned—at the very least surprised. Instead, she met him need for need. When his tongue slipped into her mouth, she responded like someone as starved for this as he was.

Heat exploded in his middle, along with a feeling so foreign he couldn't have described it to save his life. Part need, part entitlement, part something dark and wonderful, it fueled the fire in his soul and nudged him to go further, take what he wanted, salve this crazy ache that dogged him every time he was around her.

The door opened and sounds from the wedding below billowed inside. Missy jerked away, her eyes filled with fire. From passion or from anger, Wyatt couldn't tell.

She pulled a tissue from her pocket, quickly dabbed her lips, turned and faced the bride, groom and photographer with a smile.

"Come in. We're all set up."

* * *

What the hell was that?

Missy smiled at the bride and groom, leading them and the wedding party to the Eiffel Tower cake. As the crowd gushed, complimenting the detail, retelling the story of how the groom had proposed, her thoughts spun away again.

Had Wyatt kissed her out of jealousy?

Her stomach knotted. He'd absolutely been jealous. But she'd bet her bottom dollar the kiss hadn't been out of jealousy, but was meant to teach her a lesson. She'd responded to prove she was able to take care of herself. And instead...

Well, she'd knocked them both for a loop.

The question was—

How did they deal with it?

The bride and groom posed for pictures with the cake, along with their parents and the bridal party. They served each other a bite of the cake as the photographer snapped more pictures. Almost as quickly as they'd come, they left, taking the bridal party with them.

And the room went silent.

Missy sighed, calmly walking to the cake table, though inside she was scrambling for something to say. Anything to get both their minds off that kiss.

"My best cake ever and I won't be getting any referrals from it."

He didn't even glance at her. "How do you know?"

Either he wasn't happy about being jealous or he wasn't happy that this kiss had been better than their first. "Only the wedding party and the bride and groom saw it."

He sniffed a laugh. "Give people time to taste it. You'll get your referrals."

"That's just it. They didn't leave instructions to serve it." She sighed. "I'm going to find the bride's mom."

With that, she left, and Wyatt collapsed against the silent, empty bar behind him. He didn't need to wonder what had happened when they kissed. He didn't need to probe why he'd been jealous. He was falling for her. A few weeks past his divorce and like a sucker he was falling for somebody new.

He couldn't let it happen. Not just to protect himself, but to protect her. She didn't want to fall in love with a guy who wasn't ready for a commitment, any more than he wanted to fall in love so soon after he'd ended his marriage. Only beginning to get her feet wet with her business, she wanted the fun, the thrill, of stepping into her destiny. Of making money. Running the show.

Her response to his kiss had started out as a way to tell him to back off, that she could handle herself. No matter that it ended up with both of them aroused and needy. The original intent had been clear. Now he had to return them to sanity.

Though he was starving, he begged off her homemade dinner and drove ten miles to the next town over to eat meat loaf that was a disgrace. Sunday, he played with the kids but avoided seeing Missy. On Monday morning, however, he arrived at her back door as soon as he saw the kitchen light go on. He knocked twice, then let himself inside.

Without turning around, she said, "Come in, Wyatt."

The laugh in her voice told him she wasn't as afraid to be around him as he was to be around her. That served to strengthen his resolve. Wrapped up in her new business venture, she was too busy to dwell on runaway emotions the way he was. Not just the rumble of attraction, the longing to kiss her senseless and make her his, but the urge to protect her, bring her into his home…really make her his.

He knew these urges were wrong. With the ink barely dried on his divorce papers, they could simply be rebound needs. So he had to get hold of himself. To protect himself, but also to protect her. Whether she knew it or not, she was vulnerable. He could be a real vulture when he went after something he wanted. She wouldn't stand a chance.

And after he got what he wanted, he'd get bored, and he'd leave her hurt and broken.

He would not do that to her.

Since their biggest temptation time seemed to be weddings, there was an easy answer.

"This week we're going to have to find that assistant for you."

She walked away from the coffeepot, holding two steaming mugs. She handed one to him and they sat at the table, where all three kids sleepily played with cereal that swam in milk made chocolate by the little bites bobbing in it.

"Did you get any responses to your ad?"

"Lots. I'm just not sure where to interview people."

"Since you're going to be baking here at your house, I think the interviews should take place here."

"Okay." She sipped her coffee, then smiled. "Want some cocoa bites?"

"I thought you'd never ask."

They called the four candidates Missy deemed best suited for her company, and set up interviews for Tuesday, Wednesday and Thursday.

Wyatt sat with her through the interview for the first candidate, Mona Greenlee, a short, squat woman who clearly loved food. But after a comment or two at the beginning of the meeting, he stopped talking and let Missy ask her questions, give Mona a tour of the house and introduce her to the kids.

Mona laughed about how unusual it was to bake from a house, but Missy assured her that her kitchen had passed inspection. After she left, Wyatt headed for the door.

"Where are you going?"

He turned slowly. When he finally caught her gaze, she saw a light in his eyes that caused her heart to stutter. His focus fell from her eyes to her mouth, then rose again. "You can handle these interviews on your own."

Though complimented by his faith in her, she got a funny feeling in her stomach. Was he leaving because he was thinking about kissing her?

Remembering the kiss from Saturday made her stomach flip again. That was one great kiss. A kiss she wouldn't mind repeating. But they'd been attracted to each other right from the beginning and they'd managed to work together in spite of it. Wanting to kiss shouldn't cause him to leave.

"You don't want to help?"

"You're fine without me."

But I like spending time with you. I like your goofy comments. I like you.

The words swirled around in Missy's head so much, she almost said them. But she didn't. First, the intensity of her feelings surprised her, and she needed to think them through. Second, if she'd grown so accustomed to having him around that she didn't mind having him neb his nose into her business, then maybe things had gone further than she wanted them to.

He didn't want a relationship. She didn't want a fling. It was better not to encourage these feelings. And maybe he was right. They shouldn't spend so much time together.

She did the next interview alone and didn't have a problem until Jane Nelson left. Then she scurried outside to find Wyatt. Not to ask for help, but to talk. To tell him about Jane. To show him that she could handle all this alone, and how excited she was.

But when she walked into the backyard where he was playing Wiffle ball with the kids, he barely spoke to her. He complimented the job she had done interviewing Jane, but he didn't ask questions or go into detailed answers. He was distancing himself from her.

Disappointment followed her back into the house. She didn't *need* him, but suddenly everything she did felt empty without him.

At the end of the next two interviews, she didn't bother looking for Wyatt, but that didn't stop the emptiness. After so many weeks of having him underfoot, it seemed wrong that he was pulling away from her.

Except he'd be leaving in a few days. Maybe he was preparing them both?

That would be okay, except she didn't want to be prepared. She wanted to enjoy the last few days she had with him. What was the point of starting the empty feeling early? It would find a home in her soon enough, when he really did leave.

Thursday evening she offered Elaine Anderson the job. She'd blended in best with the chaos and the kids, and was able to start immediately.

To celebrate, Missy made fried chicken, and sent Owen over to get Wyatt. She knew that was a tad underhanded, but after several days of not seeing him, she was tired of wasting the precious little time they had left together. Plus, spending a few days without him had forced her to see that she liked him a lot more than she thought she did. So tonight she intended to figure out what was really going on with him.

If he was upset about their kiss and didn't want to repeat it, she would back off.

But if he was struggling with jealousy and the lines they'd drawn about their relationship, maybe it was time to change things. He didn't want a relationship. She didn't want a fling, but surely they could find a compromise position? Maybe agree to date long distance for a few months to see if this thing between them was something they should pursue.

He strolled over to the picnic table behind bouncing Owen, who was thrilled to be getting his favorite fried chicken, and in general thrilled with life these days. She no longer worried about his transition after Wyatt left. With money to put the kids in day care for four hours every morning, she knew Owen would find friends. Her life was perfect.

Except for the empty feeling she got every time she thought about Wyatt leaving.

But tonight she intended to set this relationship onto one course or another. Either ask him to work something out with her or let him go. And then stick by that decision.

"I hope you like fried chicken."

He reached for two paper plates, obviously about to help her dish up food for the kids. "I don't think there's a person in the world who doesn't like fried chicken."

Watching him help Owen get his dinner, she

pressed her lips together. There was so much about Wyatt that was likable, perfect. And she wasn't just talking about his good looks, charm and sex appeal. He liked her kids. Genuinely liked them. Plus, with the exception of the last wedding, they always had fun together. They understood each other.

Hell, he was the first person—the only person—to know her whole story. It didn't seem right that this had to end.

She put three stars on the plus column for a relationship. He liked her kids. He was fun to be around. He knew her past and didn't think any less of her for it.

They settled on the worn bench seats, said grace and dug into dinner.

He groaned with ecstasy.

She smiled. Whoever said the way to a man's heart was his through stomach must have known tall, perpetually hungry Wyatt.

"This is fantastic."

"Just a little something I can whip up at a moment's notice." Not that she was bragging, but it never hurt to remind him that she wasn't just a businesswoman and mother. There were as many

facets to her as there were to any of the women
he dated in Florida. She smoothed her palms
down the front of her shorts. After cooking the
chicken, she'd changed into her best pink shirt,
the one her former coworkers told her bought
out the best in her skin tones. And thinking of
the bikini-clad beach bunnies he probably met
in Florida, she was glad she looked her best. But
sitting across from him, acknowledging the re-
alities of his life, she fought the doubts that beat
at her brain.

How did a thirty-three-year-old mother of triplets compete with beach bunnies?

Should she even try?

Wasn't she setting herself up for failure?

They ate dinner with Owen and the girls gig-
gling happily. Owen grinned with his mouth full
and made Lainie say, "Oh, gross! Tell him to
stop that."

But Missy only smiled, glad to have her mind
off Wyatt for a few seconds. It was good to see
Owen behave like a little boy. Gross or not.

When they were done eating, Wyatt helped
her clear the picnic table and bring everything
into the kitchen. She persuaded him to help her

tidy up, delaying his visit, but she could see he was eager to go.

Fears and doubts pummeled her. He'd talked so little she was beginning to believe he'd already made up his mind. And if he'd set his course on forgetting her, wouldn't it be embarrassing to talk about thinking of a compromise for them? That kiss on Saturday, the one that had gotten away from them and knocked both of them to their knees, proved there was something powerful between them. Something she wanted. Something he seemed to be afraid of.

And even now he was straining toward the door.

Owen popped into the kitchen, already bathed. His sisters were now in the tub. With his pajama top on backward, he raced to Wyatt with a huge storybook. Big and shiny, with a colorful cover, it hid half his body.

"You wead this to me?"

"I don't know, buddy. I should get going."

Missy waited in silence. She could nudge Wyatt into reading the book, but this was a big part of what she'd want in any man she let into her life. A real love for her kids. Wyatt had shown he loved to play. He'd also shown a certain kinship with Owen. But when the chips were down, when he wanted to leave, would he stay?

He stooped down. "I'm kinda tired."

Owen rolled his eyes. "It takes five minutes."

Then the most wonderful thing happened. Wyatt laughed. He laughed long and hard. When he was done, he scooped Owen up, book and all, and carried him down the hall. "Which one's your room?"

Missy scrambled behind them. "They all still sleep in the same room. I'm waiting until Owen's a little older before I make him sleep by himself."

When they reached the bedroom, Wyatt tossed Owen on his bed. He giggled with delight.

The girls ran into the bedroom. Dressed in their pink nighties, they raced to their beds and slid under the covers.

Wyatt sat on the edge of Owen's bed. He opened the book.

"'The adventures of Billy Bunny,'" he read, and Missy leaned against the door frame, "'began behind the barn.'"

He glanced back at Missy. "A lot of alliteration in this thing."

"Kids like that…and things that rhyme."

He nodded. "Point taken."

He turned his attention back to the book. "'A curious bunny, he spent his days exploring.'"

Missy watched silently, noting how the girls laid on their backs and closed their eyes, letting the words lead them to dreamland. But Owen sat up, looked at the pages, looked at Wyatt with real love in his eyes.

And that's when Missy fell in love. Or maybe admitted the love she'd had for Wyatt ever since they'd been on his bike and she'd laid her head on his back. This guy wasn't just sexy and smart. He had a real heart. For her kids. For her—if that kiss was anything to go by.

And she suddenly knew that was why he'd been so closed off. He was falling for her and he didn't want to be. What he felt for her was about more than sex. And it scared him.

When the story ended, he shut the book. Owen had snuggled into his side, but his eyes drooped.

"Wead it again."

Wyatt rose, shifting Owen to his pillow as he did so. "You're sleepy."

"But I wike it."

He pulled the covers to Owen's chin. "And you can hear it again tomorrow."

Owen's eyes drifted shut. Missy pushed away from the door frame, smiling at Wyatt as he flicked off the bedside lamp and walked out of the room.

"Thanks."

He stepped into the hall.

She closed the door behind him. If what he felt for her was about more than sex, more than a fling, then she definitely wanted it. "Want a beer?"

He cleared his throat. "I need to get home."

"Please? Just five minutes."

He rubbed his hand along the back of his neck. "Let's talk on the porch."

On the way to her kitchen door, she grabbed two bottles of beer. She understood why he was afraid. If falling for him had scared and confused her, she could only imagine what it felt like to be a newly divorced guy falling for a woman with three needy kids. But she wasn't asking him to marry her. At least not now. All she wanted was a little time. A visit or two after he returned to his real life, and maybe the option for her and the triplets to visit him this winter.

As the screen door slapped closed behind her, she handed him a beer.

He looked at the bottle, looked at her. "We shouldn't do this."

"What? Drink? We're both over twenty-one. Besides, we limited ourselves to a bottle. We're strong, mature and responsible that way."

He let out a sigh. "That's just it. You are strong and mature and responsible. I am not."

"You think you're not, but I see it every day."

"Trust me. You're seeing a side of me that few people ever do."

She smiled. "I suspected that."

As if wanting to prove himself to be irresponsible and immature, he guzzled his beer and handed the empty to her.

"In Florida I'm moody, bossy and pushy."

"You've been pretty moody, bossy and pushy here, too, but you're also good to the kids, good to me, fun to be around, considerate."

He groaned and turned away. When he faced

her again frustration poured from him. "Don't make me into something I'm not!"

At his shout, she backed up a step. "I'm not."

"You are! What you see as good things, I see as easy steps. Who wouldn't enjoy a few weeks of playing with kids, no stress, no pressure? Even helping you with cakes and money and finding a van—those things were fun. But in a few days I go home, and when I do, I'll be back to working ten- and twelve-hours days, pushing my employees, making my parents crazy when I bow out of invitations I'd agreed to because they suddenly don't suit me." His voice softened on the last words. He reached out and gently stroked Missy's cheek. "I wish I was the guy you think I am. But I'm not." He snorted. "Just ask my ex-wife."

He took one final long look at her, then bounded off the porch, down the steps and across her yard. She stood watching him, her heart sighing in her chest.

His anger had surprised her, but the way his voice had softened and his eyes filled with longing meant more than his words. He talked about a person she didn't know. Someone impossible to get along with. He'd been a little pushy and bossy around her, but not so much that he was offensive or even hard to handle. Yet it was clear he saw himself as impossible to get along with.

So how could the guy who was so good to her kids, so good to her, think himself impossible to get along with?

Running his company couldn't make him feel that way. He'd never been anything but calm, cool and collected when discussing her business. He knew he was smart. He knew what he was doing.

Unless dealing with a scheming wife, a woman who'd insinuated herself into his company, had made him suspicious, bossy, difficult—out of necessity?

And being away from his ex and the business had brought back the nice guy he was?

That had to be it. It was the only theory that made sense.

Around his ex-wife, he'd always had to be on guard and careful, so he didn't see how good he was. But Missy did. And somehow between now and the day he left, she was going to have to get him to see it, too.

CHAPTER TEN

WHEN WYATT GLANCED OUT the window Saturday afternoon, Missy wasn't carrying a cake with Nancy, the babysitter. She and her assistant, Elaine, lugged the huge violet creation to the back of her new van.

Pride enveloped him. This week's cake was huge and fancy. Flowers made ropes of color that looped from layer to layer. It reminded him of the Garden of Eden.

But as he admired her in her pretty pink dress, a dress that complemented the cake, he realized he wouldn't be scrambling to put on clean clothes, or driving with her to a wedding reception, helping to set up, telling her how much he liked her latest cake, dancing, almost kissing— actually kissing. His breath stalled. That last kiss had been amazing.

Still, forcing her to hire her assistant quickly had been the right thing to do. He didn't want any more time with her. He didn't want to lead her on and he didn't want her getting any more wild ideas that he was a nice guy. This—her leaving without him—was for the best.

She got behind the steering wheel and her assistant jumped into the passenger's side. As Missy put the van into reverse and started out of the driveway, she called, "See you later, kids!"

He watched her leave, his heart just heavy enough to make him sad, but not so heavy that he believed he'd done the wrong thing in standing her on her own two feet and then stepping back.

He turned to face another bed full of boxes, this one in the first of two extra bedrooms. His grandmother might have been a neat, organized hoarder, but she'd been a hoarder all the same. He worked for hours, until his back began to ache. Then he glanced out the window longingly. On this sunny May afternoon, he had no intention of spending any more time inside, looking for jewelry that he was beginning to believe did not exist.

He slid into flip-flops and jogged down his back porch steps. Ducking under the shrub, he noticed the kids were in the sandbox. Nancy sat on the bench seat of the old wooden picnic table.

He ambled over. "Hey."

Owen's head shot up. "Hey, Wyatt."

"Hey, Owen." He faced the babysitter. "Can I play?"

Nancy rose from the picnic table. "Actually, I was hoping you'd come over."

He peeked at her. Sixteen, pretty and probably very popular, she reminded Wyatt of the sitters his mom used to hire when he was a kid. Young. Impressionable.

He wasn't sure he should be glad she was hoping he'd come over. "You were?"

She winced. "Tomorrow's Mother's Day and I forgot to get my mom a gift."

"Oh, shoot!" He winced with her, happy her gladness at seeing him was innocent, but also every bit as guilty as she was about the Mother's Day gift. "I forgot, too."

"I'll tell you what. You give me fifteen minutes to run to the florist and I'll order both of our moms flowers."

He waved his hand in dismissal. "That's okay.

I can do mine online. You go, though. There's nothing worse than forgetting Mother's Day."

"My mother would freak."

He laughed. "My mother would double freak."

"So you're okay with the kids? The florist is on Main Street and I can be there and back in fifteen minutes."

"If they're not crowded."

She grimaced. "Yeah. If they're not crowed."

He slid out of his flip-flops. "Take your time. We'll be fine."

When she was gone, the triplets shifted and moved until there was enough space for Wyatt in the sandbox. They decided to build a shopping center, which made Owen happy and also pleased the girls, who—though he hadn't thought them old enough to understand shopping—seemed to have the concept down pat.

After five minutes of moving sand, Owen suddenly said, "What's Mother's Day?"

"That's the day you buy your mom…" Wyatt stopped, suddenly understanding the three big-eyed kids who hung on his every word. He didn't have to do the math to know that they'd never bought their mother a gift for Mother's Day.

Their dad had been gone on their first Mother's Day. Missy's mom was dead, so they'd never seen Missy buy a Mother's Day gift. Missy's dad was worthless, so there had been no one to tell them about Mother's Day, let alone help them choose gifts.

"It's the day kids buy their mom a present—usually flowers—so she knows that they love her."

Owen studied him solemnly. "We love our mom."

Wyatt's heart squeezed. The temptation to help them order flowers was strong, but this was exactly the kind of thing he shouldn't be doing. It was easy, goofy things like this that made Missy think he was nice.

He wasn't. He was a cutthroat businessman.

He cleared his throat. "Yeah. I know you love your mom."

Lainie tapped on his knee. "So we should get her flowers."

The desire to do that rumbled through him. He didn't just want to help these kids; he also knew Missy deserved a Mother's Day gift.

Ah, hell. Who was he kidding? Wild horses

couldn't stop him from helping them. Somehow he'd downplay his role in things.

He pulled out his phone. "And that's why we're going to order some."

All three kids stared at him, hope shining from their big eyes. He looked down at the small screen before him. It seemed too impersonal to buy their first ever Mother's Day gift from a tiny screen on a phone. Particularly since the babysitter had said the florist was a five-minute walk away.

He rose, dusted off his butt. "You know what? I think we should do a field trip."

Lainie gaped at him as if he'd grown a second head. "We're going to a field?"

He laughed. "We're going to the florist." He looked down. All three kids had on tennis shoes. They were reasonably clean. He had credit cards in his wallet in his back pocket. They were set.

He caught Lainie's hand, then Claire's. "Owen, can you be a big boy and walk ahead of us?"

His chest puffed out with pride. "Yeth."

Lainie dropped his hand. "I can walk ahead, too."

Wyatt laughed. The little brunette had definitely inherited her mother's spunk—and maybe a little of her competitiveness. "Go for it."

They strode out of the drive, Claire holding his hand, Owen sort of marching and Lainie pirouetting ahead of him. Wyatt directed them to turn right, then herded them across the quiet street and turned right again.

The walk took more like ten minutes, not the five Nancy had said, and Wyatt ended up carrying Claire, but they made it.

Owen opened the door to the florist shop and a bell sounded as they entered.

Because it was late afternoon, probably close to closing time, the place was almost empty. Nancy was at the counter, paying for her flowers.

She grinned when she saw the kids. "Hi, guys." Then she glanced at Wyatt. "What's up?"

"We've decided to get flowers, too. For Missy."

Her eyes widened with understanding. "What a great idea! Do you want me to stay and help?"

"No. We'll meet you back at the house."

She kissed each kid's cheek, then headed for the door, a huge purple flowery thing in her hands.

Wyatt faced the clerk. "What was that?"

The fifty-something woman smiled. "Hydrangeas." She peered into Claire's face. "I recognize the little Brooks kids, but I'm not familiar with you."

"I'm Wyatt..." His eyes narrowed as he read her name tag. "Mrs. Zedik?"

"Yes?"

"You taught me in fourth grade."

She looked closer. "I can't place you."

"That's because I wear contacts instead of big thick glasses. I'm Wyatt McKenzie."

She gasped. "Well, good gravy! Wyatt McKenzie. What brings you home?"

"Looking through things in Gram's house. Making sure she doesn't have a Rembrandt that gets sold for three dollars and fifty cents at the garage sale the real estate agent is going to have once we put the house on the market."

The woman laughed. "And what are you doing with the Brooks triplets?"

Lainie and Owen blinked up at her.

From her position on Wyatt's arm, Claire said, "We're shopping for Mother's Day flowers."

Mrs. Zedik came out from behind the counter. "And what kind of flowers do you want?"

Lainie said, "Pink."

Claire said, "Yellow."

Owen pointed at a huge bushlike thing. "Those."

Mrs. Zedik laughed. "Well, I might be able to find the azaleas the boy wants in pink. That way two kids would get what they want."

Claire caught Wyatt's face and turned it to her. "I want yellow."

He said to Mrs. Zedik, "She wants yellow."

"So we'll pick two flowers."

"How about if we let each kid get the flower they want?" He set Claire on the floor and reached for his credit card. "Sky's the limit on this thing."

With a chuckle she took the card. "I heard you made some money."

"Yeah. And it's no fun having money if you can't use it to make people happy." He stooped to the kids' level. "Pick what you want. Everybody gets a flower to give to your mom." Then he rose. "Any chance I can get these delivered?"

She winced. "Depends on how soon you want

them. Van's out making deliveries now. Won't be back for at least two hours."

"It would be nice if she'd get them tomorrow morning."

Mrs. Zedik made a face. "We don't actually deliver on Mother's Day. It's Sunday."

"How about this? You deliver these flowers to my house this evening and I'll take care of the kids getting them to their mom in the morning."

"That sounds good."

Even as he spoke, Lainie called out, "I want this one."

Claire said, "I want this one."

Lainie looked at Claire's flower, then her own. "I want that one, too."

Mrs. Z walked up behind him. "I do have two of those."

"Okay, we'll get two of those and Owen's bush."

Owen said, "I want one of these, too." He pointed at an arrangement.

Lainie said, "I want one of those, too."

Mrs. Z's eyebrows rose.

Wyatt sucked in a quick breath. "Might be easier to let them each pick two."

"Can I have one of those?" This time Owen pointed at a vase in a cooler with a long-stemmed red rose.

"Owen, that would be three flowers."

He nodded.

Wyatt laughed.

Mrs. Z smiled. "You said money was no fun unless you spent it."

"I'm just hoping you have a van big enough to get them everything they want."

"I think it's sweet."

He didn't like thinking about how sweet it was. He'd told Missy the last time they'd talked that he was grouchy and bossy, and usually he was. But how could he resist helping her kids show her that they love her? "Actually, it's more of a necessity, since I haven't yet figured out how to tell these kids no."

Mrs. Z rounded the counter. "Just let me get a tablet and start writing some of this down."

In the end, they bought nine flower arrangements, three long-stemmed roses in white vases, three Mother's Day floral arrangements and three plants.

He walked the kids back to the house, Owen in

the lead with Lainie pirouetting behind him. But when Wyatt slid Claire to the ground again, another thought hit him. He directed them to sit on the bench seat of the picnic table, and crouched in front of them.

"Mother's Day is a special day when moms don't just get flowers, they also aren't supposed to work."

The kids gave him a blank stare.

"At the very least somebody should take them out to breakfast or lunch. So I was thinking we could—"

Owen interrupted him. "We can make breakfast."

"Yeah, we can make breakfast."

Claire tugged on his hand. "I can make toast."

"Well, that would be really cute, but it might be even cuter if—"

The sound of a vehicle pulling into the driveway stopped him. He turned and saw Missy's new van.

He rose as she got out. "What are you doing home so early?"

"Garden wedding. Fifteen-minute service.

Then an hour for pictures. Then cake and punch and we were done."

"Where's Elaine?"

"I dropped her off at home."

Missy stooped down and opened her arms. The kids raced into them. "So did you have fun today?"

"We went to—"

"We played in the sandbox," Wyatt interrupted, giving Owen a significant look. "Why don't you go wash up? At least get out of that dress?"

She glanced down at herself. "I guess I should."

"Great. The kids and I will be out here when you're done."

When she was gone, he whirled to face the kids. "The flowers are a secret."

Lainie frowned. "A secret?"

"So that tomorrow morning, we can have a big surprise. We'll hide the flowers at my house tonight, then tomorrow morning I'll sneak them over and we can have them on the kitchen table and your mom will be so surprised."

Owen frowned at him.

"Trust me. Secrets are fun." He paused to let that sink in. "Okay?"

They just looked at him.

Nancy came out of the back door and ambled over. "If you're trying to get them to keep a secret, it's not going to work. Your best bet is to entertain them so well they forget what you did today. And above all else don't say the one word that will trigger the memory."

This time he frowned. "What word is that?"

"F-l-o-w-e-r-s."

He got it. "Okay. Keep them busy, don't remind them of what we did."

Nancy ambled away, tucking her babysitting money in the back pocket of her jeans.

Heeding her advice, Wyatt said, "So, aren't we building a shopping mall?"

All three kids raced to the sandbox. When Missy came out, he kept them superinvolved in digging sand. She told Wyatt a bit about the wedding and the cake and the bride and groom, but then got bored and went into the house to make supper.

Wyatt all but breathed a sigh of relief, but fifteen minutes later she brought out hamburger patties and asked him to light the grill.

He didn't want to stay for dinner, and give him and Missy so much time together that his feelings overwhelmed him again, but he had no choice.

The girls picked up their dolls and began to follow Missy into the house. Panicking, he said, "Hey, wanna learn how to grill?"

The girls stopped, grinned and raced back to him.

Missy stopped, too, and faced him. "I was okay with you showing Owen how to light the grill, because he doesn't get to do a lot of boy things, but honestly, they're a little young to learn how to light charcoal briquettes."

"Maybe. But I don't want them to help with the grill so much as I...want to finish our shopping center."

She laughed. "Really? It's that important to you to be done?"

"We're about to lose the light."

"It's early. You have plenty of light."

"We also have lots of work to do."

She shook her head. "Suit yourself. But everybody has to wash up before they eat."

When she was gone, he directed the kids to the sandbox. "That was close."

Lainie said, "What was close?"

"Nothing." He pointed at some blocks in the sand. "Aren't you building a Macy's?"

She grinned and picked up the blocks.

All three kids got back to work as easily as if building block shopping malls was their real job. Wyatt waited fifteen minutes before he checked on the grill, found the briquettes a nice hot white and set the hamburgers on to cook.

Just as the hamburgers were getting done, Missy came out with buns and potato salad. His mouth watered.

"Are those buns homemade?"

She said, "Mmm-hmm."

His mouth really watered and he made a mental note to find himself a half-decent restaurant, because everything inside him was really liking this. And he knew he could have it, all of it, the kids, Missy, good food, if he could just pretend that he was the nice guy she thought he was.

But he wasn't.

They sat down to eat and Wyatt forced himself not to gush with praise over how delicious the food was. Then Owen unexpectedly said, "Hey, you know where we went today?"

It was everything Wyatt could do not to slap his hand over Owen's mouth to keep him quiet. Instead he said, "We went for a walk," as he gave Owen a look he hoped would remind him they weren't supposed to talk about the florist.

Owen's eyes widened, then he sheepishly looked away. But Lainie said, "I danced in the street."

Missy's head jerked up. "What?"

"When we went for our walk, I let her walk ahead of me and she sort of did those circle things ballet dancers do," Wyatt said.

"In the street?"

"There were no cars coming."

"No. But you're teaching them bad habits if you let them get too casual about crossing the street."

"Good point," he said, hoping that his easy acquiescence would smooth things over. "So your bride really liked your cake?"

Missy took a breath. Wyatt couldn't tell if it was an annoyed breath or a relieved breath.

Then she said, "Yes. The bride loved the cake." She set her fork down and smiled. "I told you I got four referrals."

"So how's your calendar looking these days?"

"Really good. I'll have to work with Elaine a lot to see if she can handle setting up a cake alone, but that's all part of being a start-up business. Everything's an experiment."

"Do you like yellow flowers?"

Wyatt's gaze jumped to Claire, who was sliding her fork around her plate as if she was bored, then over to Missy.

Missy's gaze had gone to the rows of yellow flowers around her house. She laughed. "Yes. I obviously love yellow flowers."

Claire grinned and glanced at Owen. "Told you."

Lainie said, "I like pink."

Wyatt jumped from his seat. "You know what? I think we should help your mom with these dishes."

Missy laughed. "Sit. We have plenty of time. Besides, they're paper plates. We'll toss them."

"I know, but shouldn't we get this potato salad into the refrigerator?"

She frowned. "Because of the mayonnaise?"

He didn't have a clue in hell, but he said, "Yes."

"Hmm." She rose. "Maybe."

He waved her down. "Sit! The kids and I will do it."

"Why are you spoiling me?"

"We're not spoiling you. We're—" Shoot. He almost said something about starting Mother's Day early. He wasn't any better at this than the kids.

"We know you worked hard."

Owen tugged on his jeans. "I worked hard."

"We all worked hard," Wyatt agreed. "But your mom's the only one who got paid for her work, so the rest of us are freeloaders."

Owen's face scrunched in confusion.

"Which is why we need to earn our supper by cleaning up."

Not entirely on board with the idea, Owen nonetheless got up from the table and helped Wyatt and his sisters clear away the paper plates and gather the silverware. In the kitchen, he gave each triplet a dish towel and stood over them as they dried silverware.

Missy came in carrying the potato salad. "I thought the whole purpose of getting up from the table was to bring this in."

He winced. "Sorry."

She laughed. "Your memory's about as good as mine."

They finished the silverware and cleared the kitchen table, and then there was nothing to do.

No reason to keep himself in their company.

No way he could make sure none of the kids talked about their surprise.

Owen tugged on his jeans. "You weed me a stowwy?"

Right! Story! "Only if you take your bath first."

Owen's head swiveled to Missy. "Can we?"

She frowned. "It's early."

"I never heard of a mother thinking her kids were settling in for the night too early."

Her frown deepened. "I suppose not. It's just not like them."

"Well, we did have a busy day."

She sighed. "Okay."

"Yippee!" Owen raced to the bathroom. Missy

tried to fill the tub, but Wyatt shooed her away. "I'll bathe Owen. You do the girls."

When Owen was bathed and in his pj's, Wyatt stood at the closed bathroom door, listening to the girls' chatter, hoping they didn't mention the flowers.

Apparently the promise of a story was enough to take their minds in another direction. Both Claire and Lainie raced through their baths. He smiled, listening to them talk to their mom, who told them about the bride's dress and how handsome the groom looked in his tux, making her work that day seem like part of a big fairy tale. A sweet, wonderful fairy tale where moms loved their kids and grooms didn't get divorced.

Wouldn't that be nice?

"What are you doing?"

Wyatt glanced down at Owen, who had the big Billy Bunny book again. "Waiting for the girls."

"Oh." He grinned. "I'll wait, too."

Wyatt almost argued, but with the little boy quiet beside him, he decided to take his victories where he could. When the doorknob rattled, he turned Owen toward the bedroom and they scooted down the hall. When the girls arrived in their pink nighties, he and Owen were on Owen's bed, looking as if they'd been there the whole time.

Owen handed him the book.

He frowned. "Billy Bunny again?"

"We wike it."

"Yeah," Claire said as she climbed into her bed. "We like it."

He opened the book. "Okay."

He read it twice, dragging out the story as much as he could, hoping to tire the kids. By the end of the second read through, the girls were asleep and Owen was nodding off.

When Wyatt finished, he slid out of bed, put Owen's head on the pillow and leaned down to brush a kiss across his forehead. For three kids who loved to talk, keeping their secret had probably been something akin to torture, but they'd come through like three little troupers.

He straightened away and saw Missy in the doorway, watching him with a smile. He remembered her portrayal for the girls of that day's wedding, with the handsome groom and the love-struck bride. He could almost see him and Missy standing in a flower-covered gazebo, him in a tux, her in a gown. Lainie pirouetting everywhere.

He shook his head to clear the picture. That was so wrong.

As he reached the door, he shooed her into the hall and closed the door behind him. Faking a yawn, he said, "I guess I better get going, too."

"Seriously? If I didn't know better I'd think the four of you really had been working on a shopping mall."

"Actually, I think keeping track of three kids for eight hours is harder than building a shopping mall."

She laughed, her pretty blue eyes filled with delight. "It's how I keep my girlish figure."

He glanced down, took in every curve of her nearly perfect form and swallowed hard. "You should write a book. It could be the newest diet craze. You could call it 'how to look eighteen even though you're thirty-three.'"

"You think I look eighteen?"

I think you look fantastic. The words tickled his tongue, pirouetted like Lainie across his teeth. He held them back only because he knew it was for her own good that she didn't know how beautiful he thought she was.

"Listen, I really have to go."

"Oh."

The disappointment in her voice nearly did him in. He hesitated, but gritted his teeth. He wasn't right for her. She deserved somebody better.

He headed for the door. "I'll see you tomorrow."

"Oh?"

Damn it! He really wasn't any better at this than the kids. Worse, he knew the flowers the next day would make her like him again.

He really wasn't very good at this.

That night he set his alarm for five o'clock, wanting to get up before Missy did. Still tired, he groaned when it rang, but he forced himself out of bed. Missy deserved a Mother's Day.

One by one, he carried the flower arrangements to her porch. When he realized he didn't have a key, he felt along the top of the door, looked under the mat and finally found one under an odd-looking rock in the small flower garden beside the bottom step to her porch.

He let himself in and began carrying flowers into the kitchen. With all nine pots and vases on the table, he found eggs in her refrigerator and bread for the toaster and started their simple breakfast.

Before even the first two slices of bread popped, Owen sleepily ambled into the kitchen. Claire followed a few seconds behind him and Lainie a few seconds after that.

"Everybody has to be quiet," he whispered as the kids raced to the table filled with their flowers.

Missy awakened to the oddest noise. She could have sworn it was a pop. Or was it a bang?

Oh, Lord. A woman with three kids did not like to hear a bang. She whipped off her covers and ran to the kitchen, only to find a table full of flowers, Wyatt with his arms up to the elbows in sudsy water and Claire standing on the step stool making toast.

Missy walked into the kitchen. "What's this?"

Everybody froze at the sound of her voice.

Wyatt said, "What did we practice?"

All three kids shouted, "Happy Mother's Day."

Owen raced over and caught her around the knees, hugging for all he was worth. Claire bounced off the step stool and ran over, too. Lainie danced to the flowers. "These are yours."

Her heart stuttered. Tears pricked her eyelids. She pressed her fingers to her lips. Three azalea bushes towered over the lower "fancy" arrangements, which had plastic decorations stuck among the flowers that proclaimed Happy Mother's Day! Three long-stemmed red roses sat in tall milk-glass vases.

She swallowed. Four Mother's Days had come and gone with no recognition, and truth be told, she'd been too busy to notice. If anything, she mourned her mom on Mother's Day.

She walked to the table, ran her fingers along the velvety petal of one of the roses. How could a man who thought to help her kids get her flowers for Mother's Day—a man who was making her breakfast, which she could smell was now burning—think he wasn't nice?

Her eyes filled with tears, half from the surprise and half from sorrow for him. His ex had really done a number on him.

She peeked over at Wyatt. "Thanks."

Flipping scrambled eggs, which smoked when he shifted them, he said, "It was nothing."

It was everything. But she couldn't tell him that.

This guy, who was probably the kindest, most considerate person she'd ever known, didn't have any idea how good he was.

She looked at him—organizing the kids, tossing Claire's burned toast into the trash, starting over with the scrambled eggs—and something happened inside her chest.

She'd already realized that she loved him. She'd tried a few halfhearted attempts to let him know, and even an attempt to ask him if she could visit him or if he could visit her again. But somehow she'd never been able to get out the right words. And she'd never actually led him into the will-you-visit-us or can-we-visit-you conversation.

Still, the sense she had this time, the strong sense that burst inside her and caused her spine to straighten and her brain to shift into gear, told her the days of halfhearted attempts were gone. She wanted this man in her life forever.

And by God, she would figure out a way to keep him.

CHAPTER ELEVEN

AFTER BREAKFAST, Owen and his sisters directed Missy to the living room recliner. Wyatt handed her the Sunday paper. Lainie found the side controller and flipped up the footrest.

Missy laughed. "You're spoiling me."

"Oh, I have a feeling one day of spoiling won't hurt you." Wyatt turned to the door. "We'll clean the kitchen, then get the kids out of pj's into shorts so that we can play outside."

Laughing again, she opened the paper and read until Wyatt had all three kids dressed and on their way out the door.

As soon as they were gone, she leaped out of the chair and found her cell phone.

"Nancy? It's me, Missy Brooks. Are you busy tonight?"

If she was going to seduce Wyatt McKenzie, she couldn't do it with a baby monitor in her right hand. She needed a sitter.

* * *

A little after nine that night, a knock on the door surprised Wyatt. He was in bedroom number three now. After caring for the kids that afternoon, giving Missy a break, his heart had hurt so much he'd come home and begun digging. He needed to find his grandmother's jewelry and get home before he said or did something he'd regret. Something that would ultimately hurt Missy.

The knock sounded again. "I'm coming! I'm coming!"

He raced to the door and whipped it open. There stood Missy, her hair wet from the unexpected spring rain, her eyes shining with laughter.

She displayed a bottle of wine. "It's a thank-you."

He looked at the bottle. What he'd done for her, the flowers, the breakfast, those were simple things someone should have thought to do four years ago. Yet she didn't let a kindness go unnoticed. She took the time to do something nice in return.

That was part of why he liked her so much.

Part of why she was so tempting. Part of why she was too good for him.

He opened the door and took it. "Thanks. But I'm—"

But as he tried to close the door again, she wedged her way inside. "I brought the wine for *us* to drink."

"Oh." That couldn't happen. Wine made him romantic. And after an afternoon with three kids he was coming to adore, and an emotional morning of being proud of himself for helping her kids give her a real Mother's Day, the two of them alone with a bottle of wine was not such a good idea.

Thinking fast, he said, "Well, then we'll have to drink it while we look for jewelry. That's the agenda for tonight."

She rolled up her sleeves. "I don't mind."

Of course she didn't. She might like him, but she didn't seem to be experiencing the heart-stopping, fiery attraction he had for her. Drinking wine like two friends, digging through boxes for Scottish jewelry that may or may not exist, was a fun evening for her.

Watching her, hearing her laugh, wanting her

so much he ached all over, would be an evening of torture for him.

Still, he got two glasses, pulled the cork from the wine and led her to the bedroom.

He poured two glasses of wine and handed one to her.

She peeked up and smiled. "Thanks."

His heart zigzagged through his chest. Her eyes sparkled. Her face glowed with happiness. He knew he was responsible for her happiness and part of him just wanted to take the credit for what he'd done, to accept her gratitude by kissing her senseless and—

Oh, boy. That "and" was exactly where they shouldn't go.

He turned away. "You're welcome." He put his glass to his lips, but instead of taking a sip, he gulped, then had to refill his glass.

She laughed. "I know you hate looking for this jewelry, but be careful with the wine."

"I'm not going anywhere." He couldn't keep his voice from sounding just a tad childish and bitter. And why shouldn't he be? The woman he'd always loved was at his fingertips, but he was too much of a gentleman to take her.

Damn his stupid manners! He was going to have a long talk with his mother when he got home.

"Let's just get to work."

She looked around with a smile, sipped her wine, then turned her smile on him. "Where do we start?"

"Those boxes there." He pointed at a tall stack. "Are all things I've gone through." He pointed at another stack. "So start there."

She walked over to the pile, sat on the floor and went to work on the shoe boxes, popping lids, pouring out junk, sifting through it for jewelry, and then moving on to the next box, as he'd explained to her the day her kids had helped him.

They worked in silence for at least twenty minutes. Done with her stack, she moved to the one beside it.

"I had to go through a lot of junk when my gram died, too."

Her voice eased into the silent room. Okay with the neutral comment, he said, "Really?"

"Yep. She wasn't quite the packrat your gram

seemed to be, but she kept a lot of mason jars in the basement."

He laughed. "So she was a jelly maker."

"And she loved to can her own spaghetti sauce." Missy sighed. "She was such a bright spot in my life."

"My gram was, too. That's why I moved her down to Florida with us."

"So what do you have down there to fit all these people? A mansion?"

He laughed again. "No one lives with me. I got my gram a town house and my parents have a house near mine on the Gulf."

"Sounds nice."

He glanced over. Usually when he told someone he had a house on the Gulf, they oohed and ahhed. She seemed happy for him, but not really impressed. "It's a six-thousand-square-foot mansion with walls of windows to take advantage of the view."

She winced. "You're lucky you can afford to hire someone to clean that."

His gaze winged over to her. Was she always so practical? "I don't get it very dirty."

"Was that the house you shared with your wife?"

"She got the big house."

Missy gaped at him. "She didn't think six thousand square feet was good enough?"

"She didn't think anything was good enough." He stopped himself. Since when did he talk about Betsy? About his marriage?

Missy shrugged. "Makes sense."

Cautious, but curious, because to him nothing about Betsy made sense, he said, "What makes sense?"

"That you divorced. It sounds like you had two different ideas of what you wanted."

He'd never thought of it that way. "I guess we did."

"So what was she like?"

"Tall, pretty." The words were out before he even thought to stop them. "She'd been a pageant girl."

"Oh, very pretty then."

He laughed. "Why are you asking questions about my ex?"

Missy caught his gaze. "Scoping out the competition."

He choked on his wine. "The competition?"

"Yeah. I like you." She said it naturally, easily, as if it didn't make any difference in the world. "I really like you. And I don't want to find out what to do or not do to get you to like me. I'm just trying to figure out what makes you you."

He set his wineglass down on the table. "Don't."

"Why not?"

"Because we've already been over this. My ex did a number on me. Even if I wasn't only a month out of a divorce, I wouldn't want to get involved again."

"It might be a month since you divorced, but if you fought over the settlement for four years, you haven't been married for four years."

"What?"

"You heard me. You keep saying you've only been divorced a month, but you've been out of your relationship a lot longer." She took a sip of wine. "Have you dated?"

His eyebrows rose. "I was separated. I was allowed to date."

"I'm not criticizing. I'm just helping you to understand something." She paused with a gasp. "Hey, look at this!"

The enthusiasm in her voice drew his gaze. She held up a small round thing with a woman's face on it.

She beamed. "It's a cameo."

He cautiously said, "That's good?"

"Not only does it look really old, but it's clear it was expensive." She examined it. "Wow."

He scrambled over. "What else is in that box?"

She rose, taking the box with her, and sat on the bed.

He sat beside her.

She pulled out matching combs. "These are hair combs." She studied them. "They're so pretty."

He reached in and retrieved a delicate necklace. Reddish stones and silver dominated the piece. "No wonder my mom wanted them."

"Yeah."

Missy's voice trembled on the one simple word, and even though she hadn't said it, he knew what troubled her. He set the necklace back in the box, as sadness overwhelmed him, too. "So. I found what I came for."

"Yeah. You did."

And now he could go home.

Silence settled over them. Then he peeked at her and she peeked at him. He'd never see her again. Oh, tomorrow morning after he packed, he'd walk over and say goodbye to her and the kids. But this was the very last time they'd be alone together. Once he returned to Florida, he wasn't coming back. He had a life that didn't include her, and in that life he wasn't this normal, selfless guy she was falling in love with. He was a bossy, moody, selfish businessman who now had to deal with an ex-wife who owned one-third of his company. She might not have controlling interest, but she had enough of a say to make his life miserable.

And he wouldn't waste the ten or so minutes he had with the genuinely kind, selfless woman sitting beside him, by thinking about his bad marriage.

Though Missy had paid him back for the kiss they should have had graduation night, he bent and brushed his lips across hers. He went to pull back, but she caught him around the neck and kept him where he was, answering his kiss with one that was so soft and sweet, his chest tightened.

When her tongue peeked out and swiped across his lips, his control slipped. This was the one person he'd felt connected to since he was a geek and she was a prom queen. For once, just once, he wanted to feel what it would be like to be hers. He took over the kiss, and suddenly they were both as greedy as he'd always wanted to be.

As his mouth plundered hers, his hands ran down her arms, then scrambled back up again. Her velvety skin teased him with the promise of other softer skin hidden beneath her clothes. She wrapped her arms around his back and the feelings he'd had when she'd clung to him that day on the motorcycle returned. All that trust, all that love, in one simple gesture.

She loved him.

The thought stopped him cold. No matter what he did now, she would be hurt when he left. So would it be so bad to make love, to give them both a memory?

Yes. It would be bad. It would give her false hope. It would tear him up inside to leave her.

When he pulled away, he didn't merely feel the physical loss, he felt the emotional loss. But he knew he'd done the right thing.

Missy rose from the bed. She paced around the little room as if deliberating, then swung to face him. "You know, I never felt alone. Not once in the four years after my husband left, until I began missing you."

The sadness in her voice pricked his heart. He'd deliberately held himself back the past few days. He knew that's why she'd missed him. Still, he said, "I'm not even gone yet."

"No, but you always pull away."

"I have to. One of us has to be smart about this."

"How do you know I want to be smart? Couldn't I once, just once, get something I want without worrying about tomorrow?"

Yearning shuddered through him. He wanted this night, too. And if she didn't stop pushing, he would take it. "Right from the beginning you've told me your kids come first, and the best way to protect them is to keep yourself from doing stupid things."

She faced him with sad blue eyes. "Would

making love with the first guy I've been attracted to in four years really be stupid?"

His blasted need roared inside him. For fifteen years he'd wished she was attracted to him. Now that she was, he had to turn her away. Everything inside him rebelled at the idea. Everything except the gentleman his mother had raised. He knew this was the right thing. "That's not a reason to do this."

"Okay, then." She smiled. "How about this? I love you."

The very thought stole his breath. Missy Johnson, prettiest girl he'd ever met, girl he'd been in love with forever, woman who'd made the past four weeks fun, loved him.

He'd guessed that already, but hearing her say it was like music. Still, practicality ruled him. He snorted a laugh. "Right. In four weeks, you've fallen in love?"

"What's so hard to believe about that?"

"It's not hard to believe. It's just not love. Since I've been here, you haven't merely had company, you've also had an ally for your business. Somebody who saw your potential and wouldn't let you back down or settle for less than what you deserve."

"You know, in some circles that might be taken to mean you love me, too."

Oh, he did. Part of him genuinely believed he did. And the words shivered on his tongue, begging to be released. But his practical side, the rational, logical, hard-nosed businessman, argued that this wasn't love. That everything he believed he felt was either residual feelings from his teen years or rebound feelings. Feelings that would disappear when he went home. Feelings that would get her hopes up and then hurt her.

"I care about you. But I didn't have a good marriage. And for the past four years I've been trapped in hearings and negotiations to keep my wife—ex-wife—from taking everything I'd worked for. In the end we compromised, but I'd be lying if I said I wasn't bitter. And what you think I feel—" He snorted a laugh. "Hell, what I think I feel isn't love. It's rebound. You're everything she wasn't. And I need to go home. Get back to my real life."

* * *

Hurt to her very core, Missy walked around the bedroom. There was no way she could let the conversation end like this. She picked up one of the broaches that meant so much to his family. He had roots. He'd always had stability. He didn't know what it was like to be alone and wanting. So he didn't know how desperate she was to hang on to the first person in her life she really loved. And the first person, she believed, to really love her.

"You've never once seemed bitter around me."

"That's because I've been happy around you." When her gaze darted to his, he held up his hand to stop what she wanted to say. "Or maybe it was more that around you I was occupied." He ran his fingers through his hair. "Look, I'm not going to lie to you by telling you leaving will be easy. It won't. You and the kids mean more to me than anybody ever has. But the timing is wrong. And if I stay or ask you to come with me, one of us is going to get hurt." He sucked in a breath. "And it won't be me. I'm selfish. I'm stubborn. I usually take what I want, so be glad I'm giving you a way out."

Her lips trembled. She'd presented all her best arguments and he wasn't budging. She had a choice. Stay and embarrass herself by crying in front of him, maybe even begging him to stay, or go—lose any chance of keeping him here, but salvage her pride.

She glanced up at him, saw the look of sadness on his face and knew the next step was pity. Pity for the woman who was left by her ex. Pity for the woman who was only now getting her life together after her father's abuse.

Pride rescued her. She would never settle for anybody's pity.

She softly sucked in a breath to hold off the tears, and smiled. Though it killed her, she forced her lips to bow upward, her tears to stay right where they were, shimmying on her eyelids.

"You know what? You're right. You probably are a totally different guy in Florida. I *am* just starting out. It is better not to pursue this."

"Two years from now you'll be so busy and so successful you'll forget who I am."

Oh, he was wrong about that. She'd never forget him. But he was also right. She would be busy. Her kids would be well dressed, well loved, happy. She would have all the shiny wonderful toys every baker wanted. Hell, she'd probably have her own building by then.

Still, she wouldn't let him off the hook. In some ways she believed he needed to be loved even more than she did. She loved him and he needed to know that. "I will be busy, but I won't forget you."

Her heart caught in her throat and she couldn't say any more. She turned to the door and walked out.

He didn't try to follow her.

CHAPTER TWELVE

MISSY AWAKENED before the kids, rolled out of bed and began baking. Wyatt rejecting her again the night before had stung, but the more she examined their conversation, the tortured expression on his face, the need she felt rolling from him, the more she knew he loved her.

That was the thing that bothered her about his rejecting her. Not her own loss. His. He kept saying he was protecting her from hurt, but in her own sadness she hadn't seen his loss. It took her until three o'clock in the morning to realize that to keep her from hurt he was hurting himself.

If she really believed he didn't want her, she'd let him go without a second thought. But she wasn't going to let him walk away just to protect her. Risk was part of love. Unfortunately, both of them had been in relationships that hadn't panned out, so they were afraid to risk.

Well, she wasn't. Not with Wyatt. He was

good, kind, loving. He would never leave her. And she would never leave him. She loved him.

In her pantry, she found the ingredients for lemon cake and meringue frosting. When the kids woke at eight, she fed them, then shooed them out the door to play.

As they sifted through the sand, she took a few peeks outside to see when Wyatt came out to be with them. He didn't. But that didn't bother her. He'd found his jewels the night before. He could be on the phone with his mom or even his staff, making plans to go home.

Which was why she had to get her lemon cake to him as soon as possible so she would have one more chance to talk him out of leaving, or one more chance to talk him into staying in touch, visiting her every few weeks or letting her and the kids visit him.

Elaine arrived at nine. Missy brushed her hands on her apron, then removed it. "Would you mind watching the kids while I quickly deliver this cake next door to Wyatt?"

With a laugh, Elaine said, "No. Go."

Pretty yellow-and-white cake in hand, she walked through the backyard and dipped through the hole in the shrub. Sucking in a breath for courage, she pounded up the back porch steps and knocked on the kitchen door.

"He's not here."

She spun around to find Owen on her heels. "What?"

"He just weft."

"He just weft?"

Owen nodded. "He said to tell you goodbye."

"Oh."

Wow. Her chest collapsed, as if someone had punched it. Wyatt wasn't even going to tell her goodbye? Shock rendered her speechless, but also prevented her from overtly reacting.

"Well, then let's go home. We'll eat this cake for dessert at suppertime."

Owen eagerly nodded.

But as they clomped down the stairs, the shock began to wear off. Her throat closed. Tears filled her eyes.

It really was over. He didn't want her. All the stuff she'd convinced herself of, that he loved her, that he was protecting her, it was crap.

How many times had he told her he was a

spoiled man, accustomed to getting what he wanted? How many times had he warned her off?

God, she was stupid! What he'd been saying was that if he wanted her, he would have her. And all that pain over leaving her that she'd been so sure she'd seen the night before? She hadn't.

She set the cake on the counter, gave Elaine a list of chores for the day and went to her bedroom. About to throw herself across the bed and weep, she faltered. A shower would cover the noise of her crying. Then she wouldn't have to worry about yet another person, Elaine, feeling sorry for her. She stripped, got into the shower and let the tears fall.

He might not have loved her, but like a fool, she'd fallen for him.

Wyatt had decided to take the bike home. He loved the truck, but he needed the bike. He needed the feeling of the wind on his face to remind him of who he was and what he did and why he hadn't taken what Missy had offered.

Damn it! She'd have slept with him, even after all his warnings.

He stifled the urge to squeeze his eyes shut.

A FATHER FOR HER TRIPLETS

She was such a good person. Such a wonderful person. And such a good mom.

A vision of his last five minutes with Owen popped into his head. He'd thought he could slide out the front door, zoom down the steps and get on the bike without being noticed. But the little boy had been at the opening in the shrubs. Just as he had been the day Wyatt arrived.

"Where you goin'?"

He'd stopped, turned to face him. "Home."

"You didn't give me a wide."

No longer having trouble understanding Owen's lisp, he'd laughed, dropped his duffel bag in the little pouch that made the back of the bike's seat, and headed to the opening. When he reached Owen he'd crouched down.

"Actually, I think you're too small to ride a bike."

Owen looked at his tennis shoes. "Oh."

"But don't worry, someday you'll be tall. Not just big enough to ride a bike, but tall."

The little boy grinned at him.

Wyatt ruffled his hair. He started to rise to go, but his heart tightened and he stopped. He opened his arms and Owen stepped into them.

He wrapped them around the boy, his eyes filling with tears. This time next week, when the kids went to day care, Owen would forget all about him. But Wyatt had a feeling he'd never forget Owen.

He let him go and rose. "See ya, kid."

"See ya."

Then he'd gotten on his bike and rode off.

Damn it. Now his head was all cloudy again and his chest hurt from wanting. Wanting to stay with Missy. Wanting to be around her kids. Wanting to stay where he was instead of return to the home that was supposed to be paradise, but he knew would be empty and lifeless.

Seeing a sign for a rest stop, he swung off the highway and drove up to the small brick building.

He took off his helmet and headed for the restroom. Parked beside the sidewalk was a gray-blue van. As he approached, the side door slid open and six kids rolled out. Three girls. Three boys. They barreled past him and giggled their way to the building.

"Might as well mosey instead of running." The man exiting the van smiled at him. "They'll be taking up most of the bathroom stalls and all the space in front of the vending machines for the next twenty minutes."

Last month that would have made Wyatt grouchy. This month it made him smile. He could see Missy's kids doing the same thing a few years from now. "Yours?"

"Three grandkids. Three kids with my new wife." He pointed at the tall, willowy redhead who followed the kids, issuing orders and in general looking out for them.

"Oh." Wyatt was all for polite chitchat, but he wasn't exactly sure what to say to that. The closer the stranger got to Wyatt the more obvious it was that he wasn't in his twenties, as the redhead was. Early fifties probably. Plus, he'd admitted three of those kids were his *grandkids*.

The man batted a hand in dismissal. "Everybody says raising kids is a younger man's game, and that might be true, but I love them all."

"Bet your older kids aren't thrilled."

He laughed. "Are you kidding? Our house is the in place to be. We have movie night every Friday, so every Friday both of my daughters get a date night with their husbands."

"Well, that's handy."

"And I feel twenty-eight again."

Wyatt laughed. He guessed that was probably the redhead's age.

"Didn't think I'd pull through after my first wife left me." He tossed Wyatt a look. "Dumped me for my business partner, tried to take the whole company from him." He chuckled. "My lawyers were better than theirs."

Wyatt couldn't stop the guffaw that escaped. It was nice to see somebody win in divorce wars.

"But now I have a wife I know really loves me. Three new kids to cement the deal. And very good relationships with my older kids, since I am a convenient babysitter for weekends."

"That's nice."

The older man sucked in a breath. "It is nice." He slapped Wyatt on the back. "I'm telling you, second chances are the best. Just when you think you're going to be alone forever, love finds you in the most unexpected ways." He stopped, his mouth fell open and he began racing up the sidewalk. "Come on, Tommy! You know better than that."

By the time Wyatt got out of the restroom,

the van, the older man and the kids were gone. He shook his head with a laugh, thinking the guy really was lucky. Then he walked up to a vending machine and inserted the coins to get a two-pack of chocolate cupcakes. He pushed the selection button. They flopped down to the takeaway tray.

He opened them and shoved an entire cupcake into his mouth, then nearly spit it out.

Compared to the cake he'd been eating the past few weeks, it was dry, tasteless. And made him long for Missy with every fiber of his being. Not because he wanted cake, but because she made him laugh, made him think, made him yearn for things he didn't even realize he wanted.

He wanted kids.

Someday he wanted to be the dad in the van taking everyone on an adventure. He wanted his house to be the one that hosted Friday night movie night—with the triplets' friends.

He wanted to have a bigger family than his parents and Missy's parents had given them. So his grandkids could have cousins and aunts and uncles. Things he didn't have.

But most of all he wanted her. He wanted to

laugh with her, to tease with her, to wake up beside her every morning and fall asleep with her at night. He didn't want the noise in Tampa. He didn't want to fight any more battles in courtrooms or in his boardroom. He wanted a real life.

He glanced around the crowded rest stop. What the hell was he doing here? He never ran away from something he wanted. He went after it.

And the first step was easy. He climbed on his bike, but before he started the engine, he pulled out his cell phone. He hit Betsy's speed dial number.

When she answered, he said, "Here's the deal. You come up with ten percent over the market value for my shares, or you sell me yours for their real value."

She sputtered. "What?"

"You heard me. If you want to play hardball, I'm countering your offer. I'll buy your shares for market value. If that doesn't suit you, then you buy me out. But I'm not working with you. And I'm not running the company for you. One of us takes all. The other gets lost. I don't care which way it goes."

"We're not supposed to negotiate without our lawyers."

"Yeah, well, I found something I want more than my company. I'd be happy to keep it and run it, as long as I don't have to deal with you. We never were a good match. We're opposites who argue all the time. If we try to run the company together, all we'll do is fight. And I'm done fighting. If you don't want to buy my shares, I'll find somebody who will."

She sighed. "Wyatt—"

"You have ten seconds to answer. Either let me buy your shares for what they're really worth or you buy mine and I disappear. Or I sell them to a third party."

"I don't want your company."

"Clock's ticking."

"Fine. I'll take market value."

"I'll call my accountant and lawyer."

He clicked off the call with a grin. He was free. Finally free to walk into the destiny he'd known was his since ninth grade. He was gonna marry Missy Johnson.

He started the bike and zipped onto the highway, this time going in the opposite direction, back home.

He was going to get his woman.

Missy cried herself out in the shower, put on clean clothes and set about making gum paste. While it cooled, she could have made a batch of cupcakes. Her plan was to deliver the cupcakes to every restaurant in a three-county area this week, but her heart wasn't in it. After Wyatt's rejection, she needed to feel loved, wanted. So as Elaine gathered the ingredients for a batch of chocolate cupcakes, she went outside to plant the azalea bushes the kids had bought her for Mother's Day.

The problem was she could see splashes of red through the shabby hedge. Her heart stuttered a bit. Wyatt's truck. He'd have to come home for that.

She stopped the happy thoughts that wanted to form. Even if he did come home, he wouldn't come over to see her. He'd made his choices. Now she had to live with them. With her pride intact. She didn't beg. She'd never begged. She sucked it up and went on.

She would go on now, too.

But one of these days she'd dig up those shrubs and replace them with bushes thick enough that she couldn't see the house on the other side. True, it would take years for them to grow tall enough to be a fence, but when they grew in they would be healthy and strong...and full. So she wouldn't be able to see into the McKenzie yard, and any McKenzie who happened to wander home wouldn't be able to see into hers.

She snorted a laugh. No McKenzie would be coming home. He'd probably send somebody to pick up the truck, and hire a Realtor to sell the house. She had no reason to protect herself from an accidental meeting. There would be no accidental meeting.

The roar of a motorcycle in her driveway brought her back to the present. Her first thought was that someone had chosen to turn around in her drive. Still, curious, she spun around to see who was.

Wyatt.

Her heart cartwheeled. *Wyatt.*

She removed her gardening gloves and tossed them on the picnic table, her heart in her throat.

As he removed his helmet and headed into her yard, all three kids bounced up with glee. He got only midway to the picnic table before he was surrounded. He reached down and scooped up Claire. Helaina and Owen danced around him as he continued toward the picnic table.

"Are we going to play?" Owen's excited little voice pierced her heart. This was just like Wyatt. Come back for two seconds, probably to give her keys to the truck for whoever he sent up to retrieve it, and undo all the progress she'd made in getting the kids to understand that he'd left and wasn't coming back.

"In a minute." He slid Claire to the ground again. "I need to talk to your mom."

All three kids just looked at him.

He laughed. "If you go play now, I'll take you for ice cream later."

Owen's eyes widened. "In the twuck?"

Missy sighed. Now he was just plain making trouble for her. "The truck doesn't have car seats."

Wyatt sat on the bench across from hers and casually said, "We'll buy some."

That was good enough for the triplets. With a

whoop of delight from Owen and a "Yay!" from Claire and Lainie, the three danced over to the sandbox.

"Why are you here?" There was no point delaying the inevitable. "Did you forget something?"

He laughed. "Yes. I forgot you guys."

"Right." She glared at him across the table. "What the hell is that supposed to mean?"

"It means I don't want to go back without you."

Her heart tripped. She caught herself. She hadn't precisely misinterpreted everything he'd said and done to this point, but she had done a lot of wishful thinking. She liked him. But they were at two different places in their lives. And even if they weren't, they lived in two different parts of the country.

"I shouldn't have gone."

She sniffed a laugh. "You seemed pretty certain about it last night."

"Last night I was an idiot. This morning I left without talking to you because I didn't want to hurt you. Turns out I hurt myself the most by leaving."

She shook her head. "So this is all about you?"

"This is all about us. About how we fit. About how we would be a family."

For the first time since he'd walked over from her driveway, hope built in her heart. But hope wasn't safe. She'd spent her childhood hoping her dad would change. Her marriage hoping her husband would stay with her. Every time she hoped, someone hurt her or left her.

"Hey." His soft voice drifted over to her as his strong hand reached across the table and caught hers. "I'm sorry. I shouldn't have gone. I didn't even want to leave. But something inside me kept saying I couldn't do this. That I'd hurt you and hurt the kids."

She didn't look at him. She couldn't. If she glanced over and saw those big brown eyes sad, she'd melt. And she didn't want to melt. She needed to be strong to resist whatever nonsense he was about to say.

"Then I saw this guy and his family at a rest stop on I-95. His first wife had dumped him for his business partner and he married this really hot chick who had to be at least thirty years younger than he was."

Missy couldn't help it. She looked over at him with a laugh. "Are you kidding me?"

"No. Listen." He rose from his side of the picnic table and walked over to hers. Sitting almost on top of her, he forced her to scoot over to accommodate him. "He had six kids in a van that sort of looked like yours."

"Six kids?"

"Half of them were his with his new wife."

"Half?"

"The other half were grandkids."

That made her laugh out loud. "Grandkids?"

"Grandkids and kids all mingled together, and they were having a blast."

She suddenly realized they were talking like normal people again. Just two old friends, sitting on her picnic table, talking about the daily nonsense that happens sometimes.

It hurt her heart because this was what she wanted out of life. A companion. A lover, sure. But more than that, every woman wanted a guy who talked, shared his day, shared his hopes, his dreams. And the easy, casual way Wyatt sat with her, talked with her, got her hopes up more than any apology.

If she didn't leave now, she'd let those hopes take flight and she'd end up even more hurt than she already was.

She rose. "Well, that's great."

He grabbed her hand and tugged her back down again. "You're not listening to what I'm telling you."

Annoyed, she turned on him. "So what are you telling me?"

"Well, I was going to say I love you, but you seem a little too grouchy to hear it."

She huffed a laugh. "You don't love me. You said so last night. You said you *cared* about me but didn't love me."

"Geez, did you memorize everything I said verbatim?"

"A woman doesn't forget the words that hurt her."

He caught her chin and made her look at him. "I do love you. I love you more than anybody or anything I've ever thought I loved. I got confused because I thought I wasn't ready or supposed to love. That guy in the van, the guy with all the kids and enough family to be an organizational chart for a Fortune 500 company?

He showed me that you don't have to be ready. Sometimes you can't be ready. When life and love find you, you have to grab them. Inconvenience, messiness, problems and all."

The hope in her heart swelled so much it nearly exploded. "Are you saying we're inconvenient?"

"Good God, woman, you have triplets. Of course this is inconvenient. You're starting a business here, which means you can't leave. My business is a thousand miles away. You haven't met my parents. Not that they won't love you, but it's going to be a surprise to suddenly bring three kids into their world. Especially since if we're going to make this work, I'm going to be spending a big chunk of my time up here." He shook his head. "They moved to Florida to be with me and now I'm going to be living at least half the year up here."

She laughed a bit. That was sort of ironic.

His serious brown eyes met her gaze. "But I love you. I want what you bring to my world."

"Messiness, inconvenience and problems?"

"Happiness, joy and a sense of belonging."

With every word he said his face got closer. Until when he said, "Belonging," their lips met.

This time there was no hesitation. There was no sense that as soon as he got the chance he would pull away. This time there was only real love. The love she'd been searching for her whole life was finally here.

Finally hers.

EPILOGUE

TWO YEARS LATER they got married on a private island about an hour down the coast from Tampa. The triplets, now six, were more than happy to be the wedding party. Owen looked regal in his little black tux that matched Wyatt's, and the girls really were the princesses they wanted to be, dressed in pale pink gowns with tulle skirts.

Nancy, their longtime babysitter, now a college sophomore, had been invited to the wedding as a guest, but ended up herding the triplets into submission as they stood at the end of the long white runner that would take Missy to the gazebo on the beach, where she would marry the love of her life.

She and Wyatt had decided to date for a year, then had been engaged for a year. Not just to give her a chance to get her company running smoothly, with a baking supervisor and actual delivery staff, but also to give the two of them time to enjoy being in love. Though Wyatt spent most of his time in her house when he visited, he'd kept his gram's house. He was very sentimental when it came to Missy, to their past, and especially to the picnic tables where he'd taught her how to solve equations.

"Okay, Owen, you're first."

Nancy gave him a small push to start him on his journey down the white runner to the gazebo, where Wyatt and the minister waited. Owen hesitated at first, but when he saw all the people urging him on, especially Wyatt's parents, his first grandparents, it was as if someone had flashed a light indicating it was showtime. He grinned and waved, taking his time as he went from the back of the beach to the gazebo.

Wyatt caught him by the shoulders and got him to stand still, but he couldn't stop Owen's grin. This was the day they officially became a family. A mom and dad, three kids and actual grandparents more than happy to spoil them rotten. Yeah. Owen was psyched for this.

Then the girls ambled up the aisle, more serious than their brother. They had rose petals to drop. Nancy had skirted the rows of folding chairs to get to the end of the runner and help the girls up the two steps into the gazebo.

Owen gave the thumbs-up signal. The crowd laughed.

Missy smiled. Then she pressed her hand to her tummy as she circled behind the last row of chairs to the runner. When she stood at the threshold of her journey up the aisle, she saw Wyatt, and all her fears, all her doubts disappeared.

His black tux accented his dark good looks, but with Owen standing just a bit above knee height beside him, and the girls a few feet away, waiting for their mom, he also looked like the wonderful father that he was.

She watched his eyes travel from her shoulders to the bodice of her strapless gown and down the tangle of tulle and chiffon that created the short skirt. His gaze paused at her knees, where the dress stopped, and he smiled before he raised his eyes and their gazes locked.

She walked down the aisle alone, because that's what she was without Wyatt. Then she carefully navigated the two steps to the gazebo and handed the two bouquets she carried to the girls.

Wyatt took her hands.

They said their vows and exchanged rings with the sound of the surf behind them. Then they posed for pictures in the gazebo, on the shore, with the kids, without the kids, with his parents and even with Nancy.

In the country club ballroom, they greeted a long line of guests, mostly Wyatt's friends and employees, as well as a swell of friends she'd made once she felt comfortable in Tampa.

As they walked to the main table for dinner, she guided Wyatt along a path that took them past their cake.

"Banana walnut?" he whispered hopefully.

"With a layer of chocolate fudge, a layer of almond, a layer of spice and an extra banana walnut layer at the top for us to take home for our first anniversary." She paused, her critical gaze passing over every flower of the five-layer cake.

He nudged her to get moving. "Everybody knows what you're doing."

She stopped, faced him with a smile. "Really?"

"You're judging that cake! Elaine was paralyzed with fear that she'd somehow ruin it."

"That's not what I'm doing."

He frowned, then his eyes narrowed. "So what are you doing?"

"I'm deciding if she's good enough to take responsibility for the wedding-cake division."

He gaped at her. "You'd give that up?"

"Not give up per se. I'd like to go back to baking. Let her supervise."

"Wow."

"It means I'd be home all winter."

His stupefied expression became a grin. "Here? In Florida?"

Her hands traveled up his lapels and to his neck. "It is our home."

"Our home. I like the sound of that."

"I want cake!"

Missy didn't even have to glance down to know the triplets had gathered at their knees.

She ruffled Owen's hair. "You always want cake. Just like your dad."

Wyatt smiled. "I like the sound of that."

"What? That you have a son?"

"Nope. I like that he already takes after me."

He stooped to Owen's height. "Don't worry. I'm guessing the guests won't eat even half that thing. You and I will be eating cake for a week."

Owen high-fived him. "All right."

They walked to the main table, raised enough for all the guests to see them. They settled Lainie and Claire in chairs to the right of Missy, and Owen between Wyatt and his parents.

When Owen grinned, Missy knew, of all the people at the wedding, herself and Wyatt included, her son was the happiest. He hadn't just gotten a dad and a grandpa; finally he wasn't the only man in the family.

* * * * *

Mills & Boon® Large Print

September 2013

A RICH MAN'S WHIM
Lynne Graham

A PRICE WORTH PAYING?
Trish Morey

A TOUCH OF NOTORIETY
Carole Mortimer

THE SECRET CASELLA BABY
Cathy Williams

MAID FOR MONTERO
Kim Lawrence

CAPTIVE IN HIS CASTLE
Chantelle Shaw

HEIR TO A DARK INHERITANCE
Maisey Yates

ANYTHING BUT VANILLA...
Liz Fielding

A FATHER FOR HER TRIPLETS
Susan Meier

SECOND CHANCE WITH THE REBEL
Cara Colter

FIRST COMES BABY...
Michelle Douglas

0813 Rom LP